J. C. Wilbee

Hymns for the Chapel of Harrow School

J. C. Wilbee

Hymns for the Chapel of Harrow School

ISBN/EAN: 9783744768030

Printed in Europe, USA, Canada, Australia, Japan

Cover: Foto ©Andreas Hilbeck / pixelio.de

More available books at **www.hansebooks.com**

HYMNS

FOR THE

CHAPEL OF HARROW SCHOOL.

HYMNS

FOR THE

CHAPEL OF HARROW SCHOOL.

Fifth Edition
REVISED AND ENLARGED.

FIRST EDITION, MDCCCLV.
SECOND EDITION, MDCCCLVII.
THIRD EDITION ENLARGED, MDCCCLXVI.
FOURTH EDITION ENLARGED, MDCCCLXXXI.

Harrow:
J. C. WILBEE,
MDCCCXCV.

PREFACE.

THE Editors of this Hymn Book desire to offer their thanks to the Proprietors of " Hymns Ancient and Modern," and to other persons by whose permission special hymns are here inserted.

HARROW SCHOOL,
September, 1895.

CONTENTS.

Contents.

Contents.

1.

AWAKE, my soul, and with the sun
    Thy daily stage of duty run ;
Shake off dull sloth, and joyful rise
To pay thy morning sacrifice.

Redeem thy mis-spent time that's past,
And live this day as if thy last ;
Improve thy talent with due care,
For the great Day thyself prepare.

Let all thy converse be sincere,
Thy conscience as the noon-day clear ;
Think how all-seeing God thy ways
And all thy secret thoughts surveys.

Wake, and lift up thyself, my heart,
And with the angels bear thy part,
Who all night long unwearied sing
High praise to the Eternal King.

Praise God, from Whom all blessings flow,
Praise Him, all creatures here below,
Praise Him above, ye heavenly host,
Praise Father, Son, and Holy Ghost !

Bishop Ken.

2.

I WAKE, I wake, ye heavenly choir,
　May your devotion me inspire,
That I like you my age may spend,
Like you may on my God attend.

May I like you in God delight,
Have all day long my God in sight,
Perform like you my Maker's will :
Oh ! may I never more do ill.

All praise to Thee, Who safe hast kept,
And hast refreshed me while I slept :
Grant, Lord, when I from death shall wake,
I may of endless light partake.

Lord, I my vows to Thee renew ;
Disperse my sins as morning dew ;
Guard my first springs of thought and will,
And with Thyself my spirit fill.

Direct, control, suggest, this day,
All I design, or do, or say ;
That all my powers, with all their might,
In Thy sole glory may unite.

Praise God, from Whom all blessings flow,
Praise Him, all creatures here below,
Praise Him above, ye heavenly host,
Praise Father. Son, and Holy Ghost !

Bishop Ken.

3.

NEW every morning is the love
    Our wakening and uprising prove,
Through sleep and darkness safely brought,
Restored to life and power and thought.

New mercies, each returning day,
Hover around us while we pray,
New perils past, new sins forgiven,
New thoughts of God, new hopes of heaven.

If on our daily course our mind
Be set to hallow all we find,
New treasures still, of countless price,
God will provide for sacrifice.

The trivial round, the common task,
Will furnish all we ought to ask,
Room to deny ourselves, a road
To bring us daily nearer God.

Seek we no more ; content with these,
Let present rapture, comfort, ease,
As heaven shall bid them, come and go—
The secret this of rest below.

Only, O Lord, in Thy dear love
Fit us for perfect rest above ;
And help us, this and every day,
To live more nearly as we pray.

J. Keble.

4.

COME, my soul, thou must be waking ;
  Now is breaking
O'er the earth another day :
  Come, to Him Who made this splendour
    See thou render
All thy feeble strength can pay.

Gladly hail the light returning ;
    Ready burning
Be the incense of thy powers :
  For the night is safely ended ;
    God hath tended
With His care thy helpless hours.

Pray that He may prosper ever
    Each endeavour,
When thine aim is good and true ;
  But that He may ever thwart thee,
    And convert thee,
When thou evil wouldst pursue.

Think that He thy ways beholdeth ;
    He unfoldeth
Every fault that lurks within ;
  Every stain of shame glossed over
    Can discover,
And discern each deed of sin.

Fettered to the fleeting hours,
    All our powers,
Vain and brief, are borne away :
  Time, my soul, thy ship is steering,
    Onward veering,
To the gulf of death a prey.

May'st thou then on life's last morrow,
   Free from sorrow,
Pass away in slumber sweet ;
   And, released from death's dark sadness,
     Rise in gladness,
That far brighter Sun to greet.

                H. J. Buckoll.
            (Translation from the German
               of Baron von Canitz).

5.

CHRIST, Whose glory fills the skies,
   Christ, the true, the only Light,
Sun of Righteousness, arise,
   Triumph o'er the shades of night :
Day-spring from on high, draw near ;
Day-star, in our hearts appear.

Dark and cheerless is the morn,
   Unaccompanied by Thee ;
Joyless is the day's return,
   Till thy mercy's beams we see ;
Till they pour their gladdening light
Through the darkness of our night.

Visit, then, these souls of Thine,
   Pierce the gloom of sin and grief ;
Fill us, O Thou Light Divine ;
   Scatter all our unbelief ;
More and more Thyself display,
Shining to the perfect day.

                C. Wesley.

6.

AT Thy feet, O Christ, we lay
 Thine own gift of this new day ;
Doubt of what it holds in store
Makes us crave Thine aid the more ;
Lest it prove a time of loss,
Mark it, Saviour, with Thy Cross.

We in part our weakness know,
And in part discern our foe ;
Well for us, before Thine eyes
All our danger open lies ;
Turn not from us, while we plead
Thy compassions and our need.

Fain would we Thy Word embrace,
Live each moment on Thy grace,
All ourselves to Thee consign,
Fold up all our wills in Thine,
Think, and speak, and do, and be
Simply that which pleases Thee.

Hear us, Lord, and that right soon ;
Hear, and grant the choicest boon
That Thy love can e'er impart,
Loyal singleness of heart ;
So shall this and all our days,
Christ, our God, show forth Thy praise.

W. Bright.

7.

MY inmost heart now raises,
   In this fair morning hour,
A song of thankful praises
   To Thine Almighty power ;
   And as I have begun
This day, my God, my life shall be
Begun and closed with praise to Thee
   Through Christ, Thy only Son.

For Thou from me hast warded
   All perils of the night,
From every harm hast guarded
   My soul till morning's light :
   Humbly to Thee I cry ;
Do Thou in grace the sins forgive
That anger Thee each day I live ;
   Have mercy, Lord Most High.

And keep me of Thy kindness
   From every harm to-day,
Nor let me in my blindness
   To Satan fall a prey :
   Order my course for me,
And bless whate'er I undertake,
Since I in all my choice would make
   As seemeth best to Thee.

C. Winkworth.
*(Translation from the German
of J. Mathesius).*

8.

I AM lucis orto sidere
 Deum precemur supplices,
Ut in diurnis actibus
Nos servet a nocentibus.

Linguam refrenans temperet,
Ne litis horror insonet ;
Visum fovendo contegat,
Ne vanitates hauriat.

Sint pura cordis intima,
Absistat et vecordia ;
Carnis terat superbiam
Potus cibique parcitas :

Ut, cum dies abscesserit,
Noctemque sors reduxerit,
Mundi per abstinentiam
Ipsi canamus gloriam.

Ascribed to Saint Ambrose.

9.

NOW hath arisen the star of day,
And with his rising let us pray,
That we throughout his course be freed
From sinful thought and hurtful deed.

Oh ! may the Lord our tongues restrain
From sounding strife, and converse vain ;
And from His servants' eyesight hide
The toys of vanity and pride.

May He our inner thoughts make pure,
From sins presumptuous us secure ;
Grant us to use such abstinence
As may subdue the things of sense ;

That we, when night succeeds to day
And this bright sun hath passed away,
Unspotted from the world may raise
To God, our Saviour, songs of praise.

Dean Alford.

10.

ANOTHER day begun !
  Lord, grant us grace that we,
Before the setting of the sun,
  Redeem the time for Thee.

  Another day of toil ;
  To Thee we yield our powers,
Keep Thou our souls from guilty soil,
  Through all the passing hours.

  Another day of fear ;
  For watchful is our foe,
And sin is strong, and death is near,
  And short our time below.

  Another day of hope ;
  For Thou art with us still,
And Thine Almighty strength can cope
  With all who seek our ill.

  Another day of grace
  To help us on our way ;
One step towards the resting-place,
  The eternal Sabbath day.

J. Ellerton.

11.

FORTH in Thy Name, O Lord, we go,
  Our daily labour to pursue ;
Thee, only Thee, resolved to know
  In all we think or speak or do.

The task Thy wisdom hath assigned
  Oh ! let us cheerfully fulfil ;
In all our works Thy presence find,
  And prove Thy good and perfect will.

Give us to bear Thy easy yoke,
  And every moment watch and pray ;
And still to things eternal look,
  And hasten to Thy glorious day.

Fain would we still for Thee employ
  Whate'er Thy bounteous grace hath given,
And run our course with even joy,
  And closely walk with Thee to heaven.

C. Wesley.

12.

UP to the throne of God is borne
    The voice of praise at early morn,
And He accepts the punctual hymn,
Sung as the light of day grows dim :

Nor will He turn His ear aside
From holy offerings at noontide :
Then here to Him our souls we raise
In songs of gratitude and praise.

Blest are the moments, doubly blest,
That, drawn from this one hour of rest,
Are with a ready heart bestowed
Upon the service of our God.

Look up to heaven ! the industrious sun
Already half his race hath run ;
He cannot halt or go astray,
But our immortal spirits may.

Help with Thy grace, through life's short day,
Our upward and our downward way ;
And glorify for us the west,
When we shall sink to final rest.

W. Wordsworth.

13.

GLORY to Thee, my God, this night,
For all the blessings of the light ;
Keep me, O keep me, King of kings,
Beneath Thine own Almighty wings.

Forgive me, Lord, for Thy dear Son,
The ill that I this day have done ;
That with the world, myself, and Thee,
I, ere I sleep, at peace may be.

Teach me to live, that I may dread
The grave as little as my bed ;
Teach me to die, that so I may
Rise glorious at the awful Day.

Oh ! may my soul on Thee repose,
And may sweet sleep mine eyelids close,
Sleep, that may me more vigorous make
To serve my God when I awake.

When in the night I sleepless lie,
My soul with heavenly thoughts supply ;
Let no ill dreams disturb my rest,
No powers of darkness me molest.

Praise God, from Whom all blessings flow,
Praise Him, all creatures here below,
Praise Him above, ye heavenly host,
Praise Father, Son, and Holy Ghost !

Bishop Ken.

14.

SWEET Saviour, bless us ere we go,
   Thy Word into our minds instil,
And make our lukewarm hearts to glow
   With lowly love and fervent will.
Through life's long day and death's dark night,
O gentle Jesus, be our Light.

The day is done, its hours have run,
   And Thou hast taken count of all,
The scanty triumphs grace hath won,
   The broken vow, the frequent fall.
Through life's long day and death's dark night,
O gentle Jesus, be our Light.

Grant us, dear Lord, from evil ways
   True absolution and release ;
And bless us, more than in past days,
   With purity and inward peace.
Through life's long day and death's dark night,
O gentle Jesus, be our Light.

Do more than pardon ; give us joy,
   Sweet fear, and sober liberty,
And simple hearts without alloy
   That only long to be like Thee.
Through life's long day and death's dark night,
O gentle Jesus, be our Light.

For all we love, the poor, the sad,
   The sinful, unto Thee we call ;
Oh ! let Thy mercy make us glad,
   Thou art our Jesus, and our All.
Through life's long day and death's dark night,
O gentle Jesus, be our Light.

F. W. Faber.

15.

O LORD, another day is flown ;
  And we, a lonely band
Are met once more before Thy throne
  To bless Thy fostering hand.

And wilt Thou lend a listening ear
  To praises low as ours?
Thou wilt; for Thou dost love to hear
  The song which meekness pours.

Oh ! let Thy grace perform its part,
  And let contention cease ;
And shed abroad in every heart
  Thine everlasting peace.

Thus chastened, cleansed, entirely Thine,
  A flock by Jesus led,
The sun of holiness shall shine
  In glory on our head.

And Thou wilt turn our wandering feet,
  And Thou wilt bless our way,
Till words shall fade, and faith shall greet
  The dawn of lasting day.

H. Kirke White.

16.

THE day Thou gavest, Lord, is ended,
　The darkness falls at Thy behest ;
To Thee our morning hymns ascended,
　Thy praise shall sanctify our rest.

We thank Thee that Thy Church unsleeping,
　While earth rolls onward into light,
Through all the world her watch is keeping,
　And rests not now by day or night.

The sun that bids us rest is waking
　Our brethren 'neath the western sky,
And hour by hour fresh lips are making
　Thy wondrous doings heard on high.

So be it, Lord ; Thy throne shall never,
　Like earth's proud empires, pass away ;
Thy kingdom stands, and grows for ever,
　Till all Thy creatures own Thy sway.

J. Ellerton.

17.

THOU Brightness of the Father's light,
　　O Christ, Thy holy ray
Is joy and strength to feeble sight,
　　Our never-dying Day.

Now, when the sun sinks down to rest,
　　And all his light grows dim,
To Father, Son, and Spirit blest
　　We raise our evening hymn.

Thee, Son of God, Thy creatures sing ;
　　And always, night and morn,
To Thee, of life the Living Spring,
　　Be purest praises borne.

F. J. A. Hort.
(Translation from the Greek).

18.

LORD of our life, Whose tender care
  Hath led us on till now,
Here lowly at the hour of prayer
  Before Thy throne we bow:
We bless Thy gracious hand, and pray
Forgiveness for another day.

Oh! may we daily, hourly, strive
  In heavenly grace to grow:
To Thee and to Thy glory live,
  Dead else to all below;
Tread in the path our Saviour trod,
Though thorny, yet the path to God.

With prayer our humble praise we bring
  For mercies day by day;
Lord, teach our hearts Thy love to sing,
  Lord, teach us how to pray:
All that we have, and are, to Thee
We offer through eternity.

19.

SUN of my soul, Thou Saviour dear,
It is not night if Thou be near :
Oh ! may no earth-born cloud arise
To hide Thee from Thy servant's eyes.

When the soft dews of kindly sleep
My wearied eyelids gently steep,
Be my last thought, how sweet to rest
For ever on my Saviour's breast.

Abide with me from morn till eve,
For without Thee I cannot live :
Abide with me when night is nigh,
For without Thee I dare not die.

If some poor wandering child of Thine
Have spurned to-day the Voice Divine,
Now, Lord, the gracious work begin ;
Let him no more lie down in sin.

Watch by the sick ; enrich the poor
With blessings from Thy boundless store :
Be every mourner's sleep to-night,
Like infant's slumbers, pure and light.

Come near and bless us when we wake,
Ere through the world our way we take,
Till in the ocean of Thy love
We lose ourselves in heaven above.

J. Keble.

20.

THE radiant morn hath passed away,
  And spent too soon her golden store ;
The shadows of departing day
    Creep on once more.

Our life is but a fading dawn ;
  Its glorious noon how quickly past !
Lead us, O Christ, when all is gone,
    Safe home at last.

Oh ! by Thy soul-inspiring grace,
  Uplift our hearts to realms on high :
Help us to look to that bright place
    Beyond the sky,

Where light, and love, and joy, and peace
  In undivided empire reign,
And thronging angels never cease
    Their deathless strain :

Where saints are clothed in spotless white,
  And evening shadows never fall,
Where Thou, Eternal Light of Light,
    Art Lord of all.

G. Thring.

21.

GOD the Father, God the Son,
　　Holy Spirit, Three in One,
Now our hallowed task is done,
　　And our prayer is prayed :
Listen, as to Thee we raise
This our thankful hymn of praise,
Ere the sun's declining rays
　　Deepen into shade.

One, O Lord, we meet to-day,
One in heart and voice to pray,
Soon to bend our peaceful way
　　Homeward with the sun :
May the bonds of living love
Bind us closer, as we move
Onward to our home above,
　　When our day is done.

One we meet to pray and sing
Praises to our heavenly King ;
Lord, in this and everything,
　　Make us one in Thee :
One in heart, and one in mind,
One in fellowship combined,
Seeking good in all to find,
　　Good in all to see.

One from rise to set of sun,
One in working days, and one,
When our day of work is done,
　　In our home above ;
One with those we love the most,
Praising, with the angel-host,
Father, Son, and Holy Ghost,
　　One in heavenly love.

G. Thring.

22.

THE sun is sinking fast,
   The daylight dies ;
Let love awake, and pay
   Her evening sacrifice.

As Christ upon the Cross
   His head inclined,
And to His Father's hands
   His parting soul resigned ;

So now herself my soul
   Would wholly give
Into His sacred charge,
   In Whom all spirits live :

So now beneath His eye
   Would calmly rest,
Without a wish or thought
   Abiding in the breast ;

Save that His will be done,
   Whate'er betide ;
Dead to herself, and dead
   In Him to all beside.

Thus would I live ; yet now
   Not I, but He
In all His power and love
   Henceforth alive in me.

One sacred Trinity !
   One Lord Divine !
May I be ever His,
   And He for ever mine.

E. Caswall.
(*Translation from the Latin*).

23.

FATHER, by Thy love and power
   Comes again the evening hour ;
Light has vanished, labours cease,
Weary creatures rest in peace :
We to Thee ourselves resign,
Let our latest thoughts be Thine.

Saviour, Thou hast seen to-day
How, like sheep, we've gone astray
Selfish wishes, thoughts of pride,
Secret sins Thou hast descried :
Blessèd Saviour, yet through Thee
Pray that these may pardoned be.

Holy Spirit, ere we sleep,
We with Thee will vigils keep :
Lead us on our sins to muse,
Truest penitence infuse,
Melt our spirits, mould our will,
Soften, strengthen, comfort still.

Blessèd Trinity, be near
Through the hours of darkness drear ;
When the help of man is far,
Ye more clearly present are :
Guard us, till the morning rays
Wake us to a song of praise.

J. Anstice.

24.

ABIDE with me ! fast falls the eventide ;
  The darkness deepens ; Lord, with me abide :
When other helpers fail, and comforts flee,
Help of the helpless, oh ! abide with me !

Swift to its close ebbs out life's little day ;
Earth's joys grow dim, its glories pass away :
Change and decay in all around I see ;
O Thou Who changest not, abide with me !

I need Thy presence every passing hour ;
What but Thy grace can foil the tempter's power?
Who like Thyself my guide and stay can be ?
Through cloud and sunshine, Lord, abide with me !

I fear no foe with Thee at hand to bless ;
Ills have no weight, and tears no bitterness :
Where is death's sting?   Where, Grave, thy victory?
I triumph still, if Thou abide with me.

Hold Thou Thy Cross before my closing eyes ;
Shine through the gloom, and point me to the skies :
Heaven's morning breaks, and earth's vain shadows flee ;
In life, in death, O Lord, abide with me !

H. F. Lyte.

25.

SAVIOUR, breathe an evening blessing,
  Ere repose our spirits seal :
Sin and want we come confessing,
  Thou canst save and Thou canst heal.

Though destruction walk around us,
  Though the arrow past us fly,
Angel-guards from Thee surround us ;
  We are safe, if Thou art nigh.

Though the night be dark and dreary,
  Darkness cannot hide from Thee ;
Thou art He, Who, never weary,
  Watchest where Thy people be.

Saviour, breathe an evening blessing,
  Ere repose our spirits seal :
Sin and want we come confessing,
  Thou canst save and Thou canst heal.

J. Edmeston.

26.

GOD, that madest earth and heaven,
   Darkness and light ;
Who the day for toil hast given,
   For rest the night ;
May Thine angel-guards defend us,
Slumber sweet Thy mercy send us,
Holy dreams and hopes attend us,
   This livelong night.

Guard us waking, guard us sleeping ;
   And, when we die,
May we, in Thy mighty keeping,
   All peaceful lie.
When the last dread call shall wake us,
Do not Thou, our God, forsake us,
But to reign in glory take us
   With Thee on high.

Bishop Heber and Archbishop Whately.

27.

THROUGH the day Thy love has spared us,
  Now we lay us down to rest ;
Through the silent watches guard us,
  Let no foe our peace molest :
    Jesus, Thou our Guardian be ;
    Sweet it is to trust in Thee.

Pilgrims here on earth, and strangers,
  Dwelling in the midst of foes,
Us and ours preserve from dangers ;
  In Thine arms may we repose,
    And, when life's short day is past,
    Rest with Thee in heaven at last.

T. Kelly.

28.

OUR day of praise is done ;
　The evening shadows fall ;
But pass not from us with the sun,
　True Light that lightenest all.

　Around the throne on high,
　Where night can never be,
The white-robed harpers of the sky
　Bring ceaseless hymns to Thee.

　Too faint our anthems here ;
　Too soon of praise we tire :
But oh ! the strains how full and clear
　Of that eternal choir !

　Yet, Lord, to Thy dear will
　If Thou attune the heart,
We in Thine angels' music still
　May bear our lower part.

　'Tis Thine each soul to calm,
　Each wayward thought reclaim,
And make our life a daily psalm
　Of glory to Thy Name.

　A little while, and then
　Shall come the glorious end ;
And songs of angels and of men
　In perfect praise shall blend.

J. Ellerton.

29.

AT even, ere the sun was set,
　　The sick, O Lord, around Thee lay :
Oh ! in what divers pains they met !
　　Oh ! with what joy they went away !

Once more 'tis eventide, and we,
　　Oppressed with various ills, draw near :
What if Thy form we cannot see ?
　　We know and feel that Thou art here.

O Saviour Christ, our woes dispel ;
　　For some are sick, and some are sad,
And some have never loved Thee well,
　　And some have lost the love they had :

And some have found the world is vain,
　　Yet from the world they break not free ;
And some have friends who give them pain,
　　Yet have not sought a friend in Thee :

And none, O Lord, have perfect rest,
　　For none are wholly free from sin ;
And they, who fain would serve Thee best
　　Are conscious most of wrong within.

O Saviour Christ, Thou too art Man ;
　　Thou hast been troubled, tempted, tried ;
Thy kind but searching glance can scan
　　The very wounds that shame would hide.

Thy touch has still its ancient power,
　　No word from Thee can fruitless fall :
Hear, in this solemn evening hour,
　　And in Thy mercy heal us all.

H. Twells.

30.

THE day is past and over ;
    All thanks, O Lord, to Thee ;
We pray Thee now that sinless
    The hours of dark may be :
O Jesu, keep us in Thy sight,
And guard us through the coming night.

The joys of day are over ;
    We lift our hearts to Thee,
And ask Thee that offenceless
    The hours of dark may be :
O Jesu, keep us in Thy sight,
And guard us through the coming night.

The toils of day are over ;
    We raise the hymn to Thee,
And ask that free from peril
    The hours of dark may be :
O Jesu, keep us in Thy sight,
And guard us through the coming night.

Be Thou our soul's Preserver,
    For Thou alone dost know
How many are the perils
    Through which we have to go :
O loving Jesu, hear our call,
And guard and save us from them all.

J. M. Neale.
(*Translation from the Greek*).

31.

HOLY Father, cheer our way
　　With Thy love's perpetual ray ;
Grant us every closing day
　　Light at evening time.

Holy Saviour, calm our fears
When earth's brightness disappears ;
Grant us in our latter years
　　Light at evening time.

Holy Spirit, be Thou nigh
When in mortal pains we lie ;
Grant us, as we come to die,
　　Light at evening time.

Holy, Blessèd Trinity !
Darkness is not dark with Thee ;
Those Thou keepest always see
　　Light at evening time.

R. H. Robinson.

32.

THE night is come, wherein at last we rest ;
  God order this and all things for the best
Beneath His blessing fearless we may lie,
    Since He is nigh.

Drive evil thoughts and spirits far away,
O Master, watch o'er us till dawning day,
Body and soul alike from harm defend ;
    Thine angel send !

Let holy prayers and thoughts our latest be ;
Let us awake with joy, still close to Thee ;
In all serve Thee ; in every deed and thought
    Thy praise be sought !

Give to the sick, as Thy belovèd, sleep,
And help the captive, comfort those who weep ;
Care for the widows' and the orphans' woe ;
    Keep far our foe !

For we have none on whom for help to call,
Save Thee, O God in heaven, Who car'st for all,
And wilt forsake them never, day or night,
    Who love Thee right.

C. Winkworth.
(Translation from the German
of P. Herbert).

33.

SERVANTS of God, awake
To hail this sacred day,
And in glad songs of praise
Your grateful homage pay :
Come, bless the day that God hath blest
The type of heaven's eternal rest.

Upon this happy morn
The Lord of life arose ;
He burst the bands of death,
And vanquished all our foes ;
And now He pleads our cause above,
And reaps the fruit of all His love.

All hail, triumphant Lord !
Heaven with Hosannas rings,
And earth in humbler strains
Thy praise responsive sings ;
Worthy the Lamb that once was slain,
Through endless years to live and reign !

E. Scott.

34.

L ORD of the worlds above,
   How pleasant and how fair
The dwellings of Thy love,
   Thine earthly temples, are !
      To Thine abode
         My heart aspires,
         With warm desires
      To see my God.

Oh ! happy souls that **pray**
   Where God appoints **to hear** !
Oh ! happy men that pay
   Their constant service **there** !
      They praise Thee still ;
         And happy they
         That love the way
      To Sion's hill !

They go from strength to strength
   Through this dark vale of tears,
Till each arrives at length,
   Till each in heaven appears :
      Oh ! glorious seat,
         When God our King
         Shall thither bring
      Our willing feet !

I. Watts.

35.

THIS is the day of light :
   Let there be light to day ;
O Day-spring, rise upon our night
   And chase its gloom away.

This is the day of rest :
   Our failing strength renew ;
On weary brain and troubled breast
   Shed Thou Thy freshening dew.

This is the day of peace :
   Thy peace our spirits fill !
Bid Thou the blasts of discord cease,
   The waves of strife be still.

This is the day of prayer :
   Let earth to heaven draw near ;
Lift up our hearts to seek Thee there,
   Come down to meet us here.

This is the first of days :
   Send forth Thy quickening breath,
And wake dead souls to love and praise,
   O Vanquisher of death.

J. Ellerton.

36.

THIS is the day the Lord hath made,
   He calls the hours His own :
Let heaven rejoice, let earth be glad,
   And praise surround the throne.

To-day He rose and left the dead,
   And Satan's empire fell ;
To-day the saints His triumphs spread,
   And all His wonders tell.

Hosanna to the anointed King,
   To David's holy Son !
Help us, O Lord, descend and bring
   Salvation from Thy throne.

Blest be the Lord, Who comes to men
   With messages of grace ;
Who comes, in God His Father's Name,
   To save our sinful race.

Hosanna in the highest strains
   The Church on earth can raise !
The highest heavens in which He reigns
   Shall give Him nobler praise.

I. Watts.

37.

BEHOLD, we come, dear Lord, to Thee,
    And bow before Thy throne;
We come to offer on our knee
    Our vows to Thee alone.

Whate'er we have, whate'er we are,
    Thy bounty freely gave;
Thou dost us here in mercy spare,
    And wilt hereafter save.

Come then, my soul, bring all thy powers,
    And grieve thou hast no more:
Bring every day thy choicest hours,
    And thy great God adore.

But, above all, prepare thy heart
    On this His own blest day,
In its sweet task to bear thy part,
    And sing and love and pray.

J. Austin

38.

JESUS, where'er Thy people meet,
  There they behold Thy mercy-seat :
Where'er they seek Thee, Thou art found,
And every place is hallowed ground.

For Thou, within no walls confined,
Inhabitest the humble mind :
Such ever bring Thee where they come,
And going take Thee to their home.

Dear Shepherd of Thy chosen few,
Thy former mercies here renew ;
Here to our waiting hearts proclaim
The sweetness of Thy saving Name.

Here may we prove the power of prayer
To strengthen faith, and sweeten care ;
To teach our faint desires to rise,
And bring all heaven before our eyes.

Lord, we are few, but Thou art near ;
Nor short Thine arm, nor deaf Thine ear :
Oh ! rend the heavens, come quickly down
And make a thousand hearts Thine own.

W. Cowper.

39.

POUR down Thy Spirit, gracious Lord,
   On all assembled here ;
Let us receive the engrafted word
   With meekness and with fear.

By faith in Thee the soul receives
   New life, though dead before ;
And he, who in Thy Name believes,
   Shall live, to die no more.

Preserve the power of faith alive
   In those that love Thy Name ;
For sin and Satan daily strive
   To quench the sacred flame.

Thy grace and mercy first prevailed
   From death to set us free ;
And often since our life had failed,
   Unless renewed by Thee.

To Thee we look, to Thee we bow,
   To Thee for help we call ;
Our Life and Resurrection Thou,
   Our Hope, our Joy, our All !

J. Newton.

40.

LORD, when we bend before Thy throne,
  And our confessions pour,
Teach us to feel the sins we own,
  And hate what we deplore.

When we disclose our wants in prayer,
  May we our wills resign ;
And not a thought our bosoms share
  Which is not wholly Thine.

Let faith each meek petition fill,
  And lift it to the skies ;
And teach our hearts 'tis goodness still
  Which grants it, or denies.

When our united voices strive
  Their cheerful hymns to raise,
Let love divine within us live,
  And lift our souls in praise.

Then, on Thy glories while we dwell,
  Thy mercies we'll review,
Till love divine transported tell
  Thou, God, art Father too.

J. D. Carlyle.

41.

SWEET is the work, our God and King,
　　To praise Thy Name, give thanks and sing ;
To show Thy love by morning light,
And talk of all Thy truth at night.

Sweet is the day of sacred rest ;
No earthly cares shall fill our breast :
Oh ! may our hearts in tune be found,
Like David's harp of solemn sound.

Our souls shall triumph in the Lord,
And bless Him for His works and word :
Thy works of grace, how bright they shine !
How deep Thy counsels, how divine !

In that eternal world of joy
Shall every power find sweet employ :
Then shall we see, and hear, and know
All we desired or wished below.

I. Watts.

42.

I N Thy presence we appear ;
   Lord, we love to worship here :
Here Thy faithful people meet
Thee upon Thy mercy-seat.

While to Thee our prayers ascend,
Let Thine ear in love attend :
Hear us when Thy Spirit pleads ;
Hear, for Jesus intercedes.

While Thy glorious Name is sung,
Touch our lips, unloose our tongue ;
Then our joyful souls shall bless
Thee, the Lord our Righteousness.

While Thy ministers proclaim
Peace and pardon through Thy Name,
In their voices let us own
Jesus speaking from His throne.

J. Montgomery.

43.

O LORD, how joyful 'tis to see
 The brethren join in love to Thee !
On Thee alone their heart relies,
Their only strength Thy grace supplies.

How sweet, within Thy holy place,
With one accord to sing Thy grace ;
Besieging Thine attentive ear
With all the force of fervent prayer !

Oh ! may we love the house of God,
Of peace and joy the blest abode ;
Oh ! may no angry strife destroy
That sacred peace, that holy joy.

The world without may rage, but we
Will only cling more close to Thee,
With hearts to Thee more wholly given,
More weaned from earth, more fixed on heaven.

Lord, shower upon us from above
The sacred gift of mutual love ;
Each other's wants may we supply,
And reign together in the sky.

J. Chandler.

44.

GREAT Shepherd of Thy people, hear,
  Thy presence now display ;
As Thou hast given a place for prayer,
  So give us hearts to pray.

Within these walls let holy peace
  And love and concord dwell ;
Here give the troubled conscience ease,
  The wounded spirit heal.

May we in faith receive Thy word,
  In faith present our prayers ;
And in the presence of our Lord
  Unbosom all our cares.

The hearing ear, the seeing eye,
  The contrite heart bestow ;
And shine upon us from on high,
  That we in grace may grow.

J. Newton.

45.

MOST glorious Lord of Life, that on this day
Didst make Thy triumph over death and sin ;
And having harrowed hell didst bring away
Captivity thence captive, us to win :

This joyous day, dear Lord, with joy begin ;
And grant that we, for whom Thou wouldest die,
Being with Thy dear blood clean washed from sin,
May live for ever in felicity.

E. Spenser.

46.

E RE another Sabbath's close,
　　Ere again we seek repose,
Lord, our song ascends to Thee,
At Thy feet we bow the knee.

For the mercies of the day,
For this rest upon our way,
Thanks to Thee alone be given,
Lord of earth and King of heaven.

Cold our services have been,
Mingled every prayer with sin :
But Thou canst and wilt forgive ;
By Thy grace alone we live.

While this thorny path we tread,
May Thy love our footsteps lead ;
When our journey here is past,
May we rest with Thee at last.

Let these earthly Sabbaths prove
Foretastes of our joys above ;
While their steps Thy pilgrims bend
To the rest which knows no end.

47.

AGAIN, as evening's shadow falls,
  We gather in these hallowed walls
And vesper hymn and vesper prayer
Rise mingling on the holy air.

May struggling hearts that seek release
Here find the rest of God's own peace ;
And, strengthened here by hymn and prayer,
Lay down the burden and the care.

O God, our Light, to Thee we bow ;
Within all shadows standest Thou :
Give deeper calm than night can bring,
Give sweeter songs than lips can sing.

Life's tumult we must meet again,
We cannot at the shrine remain ;
But in the spirit's secret cell
May hymn and prayer for ever dwell.

S. Longfellow.

48.

SAVIOUR, again to Thy dear Name we raise
    With one accord our parting hymn of praise ;
We stand to bless Thee ere our worship cease,
Then lowly kneeling wait Thy word of peace.

Grant us Thy peace upon our homeward way ;
With Thee began, with Thee shall end the day ;
Guard Thou the lips from sin, the hearts from shame,
That in this house have called upon Thy Name.

Grant us Thy peace, Lord, through the coming night,
Turn Thou for us its darkness into light ;
From harm and danger keep Thy children free,
For dark and light are both alike to Thee.

Grant us Thy peace throughout our earthly life,
Our balm in sorrow, and our stay in strife ;
Then, when Thy voice shall bid our conflicts cease,
Call us, O Lord, to Thine eternal peace.

J. Ellerton.

49.

ALL people that on earth do dwell,
   Sing to the Lord with cheerful voice ;
Him serve with fear, His praise forth tell,
   Come ye before Him and rejoice.

The Lord, ye know, is God indeed ;
   Without our aid He did us make :
We are His flock, He doth us feed,
   And for His sheep He doth us take.

Oh ! enter then His gates with praise,
   Approach with joy His courts unto ;
Praise, laud, and bless His Name always,
   For it is seemly so to do.

For why? The Lord our God is good,
   His mercy is for ever sure ;
His truth at all-times firmly stood,
   And shall from age to age endure.

W. Kethe.

50.

BEFORE Jehovah's awful throne,
　　Ye nations, bow with sacred joy ;
Know that the Lord is God alone,
　　He can create, and He destroy.

His sovereign power, without our aid,
　　Made us of clay, and formed us men ;
And when like wandering sheep we strayed,
　　He brought us to His fold again.

We'll crowd Thy gates with thankful songs,
　　High as the heavens our voices raise ;
And earth with her ten thousand tongues
　　Shall fill Thy courts with sounding praise.

Wide as the world is Thy command,
　　Vast as eternity Thy love ;
Firm as a rock Thy truth shall stand,
　　When rolling years shall cease to move.

I. Watts and J. Wesley.

51.

HARK the glad sound ! the Saviour comes,
   The Saviour promised long ;
Let every heart prepare a throne,
   And every voice a song.

He comes, the prisoners to release
   In Satan's bondage held ;
The gates of brass before Him burst,
   The iron fetters yield.

He comes, from thickest films of vice
   To clear the mental ray,
And on the eyelids of the blind
   To pour celestial day.

He comes, the broken heart to bind,
   The contrite soul to cure,
And with the treasures of His grace
   To bless the humble poor.

Our glad Hosannas, Prince of Peace,
   Thy welcome shall proclaim ;
And heaven's eternal arches ring
   With Thy belovèd Name.

                 P. Doddridge.

52.

O GLORY of Thy chosen race,
  Light of the nations, show Thy face ;
We wait in faith Thy lowly birth,
God's glory veiled to bless the earth.

Thee, Son of God, from heaven's high seat,
Thee, Virgin-born, we long to greet :
Redeemed by Thee, all worlds proclaim
The wonder of Thy twofold Name.

This earth hath seen Thy sojourn, Lord,
Who now art high in heaven adored ;
In hell's dim vale Thy footsteps trod ;
The star-worlds hymned Thee back to God.

O mighty Saviour, King divine,
Subdue this realm of flesh made Thine :
Its feeble frame cries out for Thee ;
Thy touch, Thy life, alone make free.

E'en now Thy manger gleams afar,
To waiting eyes a morning star :
In earth's dark night to faith below
Its light unquenched shall ever glow.

All praise to God the Father be,
All praise, Eternal Son, to Thee,
Whom with the Spirit we adore,
One God, both now and evermore !

F. J. A. Hort.
(*Translation from the German
of J. Franck*).

53.

JESUS shall reign where'er the sun
　　Doth his successive journeys run ;
His kingdom stretch from shore to shore,
Till moons shall wax and wane no more.

For Him shall endless prayer be made,
And princes throng to crown His head ;
His Name, like sweet perfume, shall rise
With every morning sacrifice :

People and realms of every tongue
Dwell on His love with sweetest song ;
And infant voices shall proclaim
Their early blessings on His Name.

Blessings abound where'er He reigns ;
The prisoner leaps to lose his chains ;
The weary find eternal rest,
And all the sons of want are blest.

Let every creature rise and bring
Peculiar honours to our King ;
Angels descend with songs again,
And earth repeat the loud Amen.

I. Watts.

54.

WHEN Christ came down on earth of old,
　　He took our nature poor and low;
He wore no form of angel mould,
　But shared our weakness and our woe.

But when He cometh back once more,
　Then shall be set the great white throne;
And earth and heaven shall flee before
　The face of Him that sits thereon.

O Son of God, in glory crowned,
　The Judge ordained of quick and dead;
O Son of Man, so pitying found
　For all the tears Thy people shed;

Be with us in that awful hour,
　And by Thy crown, and by Thy grave,
By all Thy love, and all Thy power,
　In that great Day of Judgment save.

C. F. Alexander.

55.

HARK! a thrilling voice is sounding,
  "Christ is nigh," it seems to say ;
"Cast away the works of darkness,
  O ye children of the day!"

Startled by the solemn warning,
  Let the earth-bound soul arise ;
Christ, our Sun, all clouds dispelling,
  Shines upon the morning skies.

Once the Lamb, so long expected,
  Came in great humility :
Once again behold He cometh,
  Robed in dreadful majesty.

Hark! a thrilling voice is sounding,
  "Christ is nigh," it seems to say ;
"Cast away the works of darkness,
  O ye children of the day!"

E. Caswall.
(Translation from the Latin).

56.

LO! He comes, with clouds descending,
  Once for favoured sinners slain ;
Thousand thousand saints attending
  Swell the triumph of His train :
      Alleluia !
  God appears, on earth to reign.

Every eye shall now behold Him,
  Robed in dreadful majesty :
Those who set at nought and sold Him,
  Pierced, and nailed Him to the Tree,
      Deeply wailing,
  Shall the true Messiah see.

Now Redemption, long expected,
  See in solemn pomp appear ;
All His saints, by man rejected,
  Now shall meet Him in the air :
      Alleluia !
  See the Day of God appear.

Yea, Amen ! let all adore Thee,
  High on Thine eternal throne ;
Saviour, take the power and glory ;
  Claim the kingdom for Thine own :
      Oh ! come quickly,
  Thou shalt reign, and Thou alone.

J. Cennick, C. Wesley, and M. Madan.

57.

HOSANNA to the living Lord !
    Hosanna to the Incarnate Word !
To Christ, Creator, Saviour, King,
Let Earth, let Heaven Hosanna sing !
    Hosanna ! Lord ! Hosanna in the highest !

Hosanna, Lord ! Thine angels cry ;
Hosanna, Lord ! Thy saints reply ;
Above, beneath us, and around,
The dead and living swell the sound :
    Hosanna ! Lord ! Hosanna in the highest !

O Saviour, with protecting care
Return to this Thy house of prayer,
Where we Thy parting promise claim,
Assembled in Thy sacred Name.
    Hosanna ! Lord ! Hosanna in the highest !

But, chiefest, in our cleansèd breast,
Eternal, bid Thy Spirit rest ;
And make our secret soul to be
A temple pure, and worthy Thee.
    Hosanna ! Lord ! Hosanna in the highest !

So, in the last and dreadful Day,
When earth and heaven shall melt away,
Thy flock, redeemed from sinful stain,
Shall swell the sound of praise again :
    Hosanna ! Lord ! Hosanna in the highest !

Bishop Heber.

58.

DIES irae, dies illa
    Solvet saeclum in favilla,
Crucis explicans vexilla.

Quantus tremor est futurus,
Quando Judex est venturus
Cuncta stricte discussurus.

Tuba, mirum spargens sonum
Per sepulcra regionum,
Coget omnes ante Thronum.

Liber scriptus proferetur,
In quo totum continetur
De quo mundus judicetur.

Judex ergo quum sedebit,
Quidquid latet apparebit,
Nil inultum remanebit.

Quid sum miser tum dicturus,
Quem patronum rogaturus,
Quum vix justus sit securus?

Recordare, Jesu pie,
Quod sum causa Tuae viae,
Ne me perdas illa die.

Quaerens me sedisti lassus,
Redemisti Crucem passus :
Tantus labor ne sit cassus.

Oro supplex et acclinis,
Cor contritum quasi cinis :
Gere curam mei finis.

Thomas of Celano.

59.

THAT Day of wrath, that dreadful Day,
   When heaven and earth shall pass away!
What power shall be the sinner's stay?
How shall he meet that dreadful Day?

When, shrivelling like a parchèd scroll,
The flaming heavens together roll;
When louder yet, and yet more dread,
Swells the high trump that wakes the dead;

Oh! on that Day, that wrathful Day,
When man to judgment wakes from clay,
Be Thou the trembling sinner's stay,
Though heaven and earth shall pass away.

Sir Walter Scott.

60.

DAY of wrath, O dreadful Day !
　　When this world shall pass away,
And the heavens together roll,
Shrivelling like a parchèd scroll,
Long foretold by saint and sage,
David's harp and Sibyl's page.

Day of terror, Day of doom,
When the Judge at last shall come !
Through the deep and silent gloom,
Shrouding every human tomb,
Shall the Archangel's trumpet-tone
Summon all before the throne.

Then shall nature stand aghast,
Death himself be overcast ;
Then, at her Creator's call,
Near and distant, great and small,
Shall the whole Creation rise,
Waiting for the great Assize.

Then the writing shall be read
Which shall judge the quick and dead ;
Then the Lord of all our race
Shall appoint to each his place ;
Every wrong shall be set right,
Every secret brought to light.

Then, in that tremendous Day,
When heaven and earth shall pass away,
What shall I, the sinner, say?
What shall be the sinner's stay?
When the righteous shrinks for fear,
How shall my frail soul appear?

King of kings, enthroned on high
In Thine awful majesty,
Thou Who of Thy mercy free,
Savest those who saved shall be,
In Thy boundless charity,
Fount of pity, save Thou me.

Oh ! remember, Saviour dear,
What the cause that brought Thee here ;
All Thy long and perilous way
Was for me who went astray :
When that day at last is come,
Call, oh ! call the wanderer home.

Thou in search of me didst sit
Weary with the noon-day heat ;
Thou to save my soul hast borne
Cross and grief and hate and scorn :
Oh ! may all that toil and pain
Not be wholly spent in vain.

Righteous Judge, to Whom belongs
Vengeance for all earthly wrongs,
Grant forgiveness, Lord, at last,
Ere the dread account be past :
Lo ! my sighs, my guilt, my shame !
Spare me for Thine own great Name !

Thou Who bad'st the sinner cease
From her tears, and go in peace ;
Thou Who to the dying thief
Spakest pardon and relief ;
Thou, O Lord, to me hast given,
Even to me, the hope of heaven.

Dean Stanley.

61.

GREAT God ! what do I see and hear?
  The end of things created ;
The Judge of mankind doth appear,
  On clouds of glory seated :
The trumpet sounds, the graves restore
The dead which they contained before ;
  Prepare, my soul, to meet Him.

The dead in Christ shall first arise,
  At the last trumpet's sounding,
Caught up to meet Him in the skies,
  With joy their Lord surrounding :
No gloomy fears their souls dismay,
His presence sheds eternal day
  On those prepared to meet Him.

But sinners, filled with guilty fears,
  Behold His wrath prevailing ;
For they shall rise, and find their tears
  And sighs are unavailing :
The day of grace is past and gone ;
Trembling they stand before the throne,
  All unprepared to meet Him.

Oh ! who may dare, just King of kings,
  To stand at Thine appearing ?
One wondrous sight my comfort brings,
  The Judge my nature wearing :
Beneath His Cross I view the Day
When heaven and earth shall pass away,
  And thus prepare to meet Him.

W. B. Collyer and T. Cotterill.
(Translation from the German
of B. Ringwaldt).

62.

THY kingdom come, O God !
  Thy rule, O Christ, begin !
Break with Thine iron rod
  The tyrannies of sin.

Where is Thy reign of peace,
  And purity, and love ?
When shall all hatred cease,
  As in the realms above ?

When comes the promised time
  That war shall be no more,
And lust, oppression, crime
  Shall flee Thy face before ?

We pray Thee, Lord, arise,
  And come in Thy great might ;
Revive our longing eyes,
  Which languish for Thy sight.

Men scorn Thy sacred Name,
  And wolves devour Thy fold ;
By many deeds of shame
  We learn that love grows cold.

O'er heathen lands afar
  Thick darkness broodeth yet ;
Arise, O morning Star,
  Arise, and never set !

L. Hensley.

63.

HARK! 'tis the watchman's cry,
    Wake, brethren, wake!
Jesus our Lord is nigh;
    Wake, brethren, wake!
Sleep is for sons of night;
Ye are children of the light;
Yours is the glory bright:
    Wake, brethren, wake!

Call to each waking band,
    Watch, brethren, watch!
Clear is our Lord's command,
    Watch, brethren, watch!
Be ye as they that wait
Always at the Bridegroom's gate:
    E'en though He tarry late,
    Watch, brethren, watch!

Hear we the Saviour's voice,
    Pray, brethren, pray!
Would ye His heart rejoice?
    Pray, brethren, pray!
Sin calls for constant fear;
Weakness needs the Strong One near:
    Long as ye struggle here,
    Pray, brethren, pray!

Now sound the final chord,
    Praise, brethren, praise!
Thrice holy is our Lord;
    Praise, brethren, praise!
What more befits the tongues
Soon to join the angels' songs,
    While heaven the note prolongs,
    Praise, brethren praise?

64.

WAKE! awake! for night is flying;
   The watchmen on the heights are crying:
  Awake, Jerusalem, at last!
Midnight hears the welcome voices,
And at the thrilling cry rejoices:
   Come forth, ye virgins, night is past;
    The Bridegroom comes, awake!
    Your lamps with gladness take;
     Alleluia!
And for His marriage feast prepare,
For ye must go to meet Him there.

Zion hears the watchmen singing,
And all her heart with joy is springing;
  She wakes, she rises from her gloom:
For her Lord comes down all glorious,
The strong in grace, in truth victorious;
  Her Star is risen, her Light is come:
   Ah, come, Thou blessèd Lord,
   O Jesu, living Word!
    Alleluia!
We follow, till the halls we see
Where Thou hast bid us sup with Thee.

C. Winkworth.
(*Translation from the German
of P. Nicolai*).

65.

MARK the seer! He cries, "Repentance!
    For the Kingdom comes apace :"
Thousands catch each burning sentence,
    Thronging to that lonely place.

'Tis the true long-sought Elias,
    By the Jordan's holy stream
Ushering in the great Messias,
    Who His Israel shall redeem.

Into those swift healing waters,
    Hoping thus their sin to end,
Israel's guilty sons and daughters,
    Conscience-stricken crowds, descend.

He, the while, Whom they expected,
    Meek, unknown, was standing by,
Soon to be by all rejected —
    "Crucify Him, crucify !"

Lord, we know Thee, and we love Thee,
    Let us not like them be blind :
Countless generations prove Thee
    Friend, Redeemer of mankind.

E. H. Bradby.

66.

BLOW ye the trumpet, blow,
　　The gladly solemn sound ;
Let all the nations know,
　　To earth's remotest bound :
The year of Jubilee is come ;
Return, ye ransomed sinners, home !

　Jesus, our great High Priest,
　　　Hath full atonement made :
　Ye weary spirits, rest ;
　　　Ye mournful souls, be glad :
The year of Jubilee is come ;
Return, ye ransomed sinners, home !

　Extol the Lamb of God,
　　　The all-atoning Lamb ;
　Redemption in His blood
　　　Throughout the world proclaim :
The year of Jubilee is come ;
Return, ye ransomed sinners, home !

　Ye slaves of sin and hell,
　　　Your liberty receive ;
　And safe in Jesus dwell,
　　　And blest in Jesus live :
The year of Jubilee is come ;
Return, ye ransomed sinners, home !

　The Gospel trumpet hear,
　　　The news of heavenly grace ;
　And, saved from earth, appear
　　　Before your Saviour's face :
The year of Jubilee is come ;
Return, ye ransomed sinners, home !

C. Wesley.

67.

BLESSÈD Lord, Who, till the morning
    Of Thine Advent shall appear,
Words of hope hast left, a warning,
    Souls to strengthen, guide, and cheer ;
Left them written for our learning,
    Pointing out the narrow way,
Lest our hearts, with all their yearning
    After home, should go astray :

Grant us, in those sacred pages,
    Grace to find the gifts untold,
Which for ages upon ages
    Did Thy people's hearts uphold :
Grant us in the sacred story
    Of the deeds which Thou hast done'
Grace to catch those gleams of glory
    That on saint and martyr shone.

Grant us faithful hearts to linger
    O'er the steps which Thou hast trod,
While Thy Cross with silent finger
    Points the upward way to God ;
With our lamps well trimmed and burning,
    Patient through Thy holy Word,
Watching for Thy bright returning,
    Waiting for our absent Lord.

J. S. B. Monsell.

68.

O SAVIOUR, is Thy promise fled?
　　Nor longer might Thy grace endure,
To heal the sick, and raise the dead,
　　And preach Thy gospel to the poor?

Come, Jesus, come! return again;
　　With brighter beam Thy servants bless,
Who long to feel Thy perfect reign,
　　And share Thy kingdom's happiness.

A feeble race, by passion driven,
　　In darkness and in doubt we roam,
And lift our anxious eyes to heaven,
　　Our hope, our harbour, and our home.

Yet, 'mid the wild and wintry gale,
　　When Death rides darkly o'er the sea,
And strength and earthly daring fail,
　　Our prayers, Redeemer, rest on Thee.

Come, Jesus, come! and, as of yore
　　The prophet went to clear Thy way,
A harbinger Thy feet before,
　　A dawning to Thy brighter day;

So now may grace with heavenly shower
　　Our stony hearts for truth prepare;
Sow in our souls the seed of power,
　　Then come and reap Thy harvest there.

Bishop Heber.

69.

RETURN, and come to God,
  Cast all your sins away:
Seek ye the Saviour's cleansing blood ;
  Repent, believe, obey !

Say not ye cannot come ;
  For Jesus bled, and died,
That none who ask in humble faith
  Should ever be denied.

Say not ye will not come ;
  'Tis God vouchsafes to call ;
And fearful will their end be found
  On whom His wrath shall fall.

Come, then, whoever will,
  Come, while 'tis called to-day :
Seek ye the Saviour's cleansing blood ;
  Repent, believe, obey!

Bishop Doane.

70.

ON Jordan's bank the Baptist's cry
    Announces that the Lord is nigh ;
Awake, and hearken, for he brings
Glad tidings of the King of kings.

Then cleansed be every breast from sin ;
Make straight the way for God within ;
Prepare we in our hearts a home,
Where such a mighty Guest may come.

For Thou art our Salvation, Lord,
Our Refuge, and our great Reward ;
Without Thy grace we waste away,
Like flowers that wither and decay.

To heal the sick stretch out Thine hand,
And bid the fallen sinner stand ;
Shine forth, and let Thy light restore
Earth's own true loveliness once more.

All praise, Eternal Son, to Thee
Whose Advent doth Thy people free,
Whom with the Father we adore
And Holy Ghost for evermore!

J. Chandler.
(*Translation from the Latin*).

71.

A VOICE by Jordan's shore!
  A summons stern and clear;
Reform, be just, and sin no more,
  God's judgment draweth near.

A voice by Galilee,
  A holier voice I hear;
Love God, thy neighbour love, for see,
  God's mercy draweth near.

O voice of duty, still
  Speak forth; I hear with awe;
In thee I own the sovereign will,
  Obey the sovereign law.

Thou higher voice of love,
  Yet speak thy word in me;
Through duty let me upward move
  To thy pure liberty.

S. Longfellow.

72.

COME, Thou Saviour long expected,
　　Born to set Thy people free ;
From our guilt and fear protected,
　　We shall find our rest in Thee.
Israel's Strength and Consolation,
　　Hope of all the saints Thou art ;
Blest Desire of every nation,
　　Joy of every longing heart.

Born the chains of sin to sever,
　　Born a Child and yet a King,
Born to reign in us for ever,
　　Now Thy gracious kingdom bring ;
By Thine own eternal Spirit
　　Rule in all our hearts alone ;
By Thine all-sufficient merit
　　Raise us to Thy glorious throne.

C. Wesley.

73.

THE Lord will come, the earth shall quake,
    The hills their fixèd seat forsake ;
And, withering, from the vault of night
The stars withdraw their feeble light.

The Lord will come, but not the same
As once in lowly form He came,
A silent Lamb to slaughter led,
The bruised, the suffering, and the dead.

The Lord will come, a dreadful Form,
With wreath of flame and robe of storm,
On cherub wings and wings of wind,
Anointed Judge of human kind.

Can this be He Who wont to stray
A pilgrim on the world's highway,
By power oppressed, and mocked by pride?
O God, is this the Crucified?

Go, tyrants, to the rocks complain,
Go, seek the mountains cleft in vain ;
But Faith, victorious o'er the tomb,
Shall sing for joy, "The Lord is come !"

Bishop Heber.

74.

WHEN brothers part for manhood's race,
What gift may most endearing prove,
To keep fond memory in her place,
And certify a brother's love?

Who art thou that would'st grave thy name
Thus deeply in a brother's heart?
Look on this saint, and learn to frame
Thy love-charm with true Christian art.

First seek thy Saviour out, and dwell
Beneath the shadow of His roof,
Till thou have scanned His features well,
And known Him for the Christ by proof.

Then, potent with the spell of heaven,
Go, and thine erring brother gain;
Entice him home to be forgiven,
Till he too see his Saviour plain.

No fading frail memorial give
To soothe his soul when thou art gone,
But wreaths of hope for aye to live,
And thoughts of good together done;

That so before the judgment-seat,
Though changed and glorified each face,
Not unremembered ye may meet,
For endless ages to embrace.

J. Keble.

75.

JESUS calls us ; o'er the tumult
    Of our life's tempestuous sea,
Day by day His sweet voice soundeth,
    Saying, " Christian, follow Me ! "

As of old Saint Andrew heard it
    By the Galilean lake,
Turned from home, and toil, and kindred,
    Leaving all for His dear sake.

Jesus calls us, from the worship
    Of the vain world's golden store,
From each idol that would keep us,
    Saying, " Christian, love Me more ! "

In our joys and in our sorrows,
    Days of toil and hours of ease,
Still He calls, 'midst cares and pleasures,
    " Christian, love Me more than these ! "

Jesus calls us ; by Thy mercies,
    Saviour, may we hear Thy call,
Give our hearts to Thine obedience,
    Serve and love Thee best of all.

                        C. F. Alexander.

76.

HOW oft, O Lord, Thy face hath shone
 On doubting souls whose wills were true !
Thou Christ of Cephas and of John,
 Thou art the Christ of Thomas too.

He loved Thee well, and calmly said,
 "Come, let us go, and die with Him."
Yet, when Thine Easter news was spread,
 'Mid all its light his eyes were dim.

His brethren's word he would not take,
 But craved to touch those hands of Thine :
The bruisèd reed Thou didst not break ;
 He saw, and hailed His Lord Divine.

He saw Thee risen ; at once he rose
 To full belief's unclouded height ;
And still through his confession flows
 To Christian souls Thy life and light.

O Saviour, make Thy presence known
 To all who doubt Thy Word and Thee ;
And teach them in that Word alone
 To find the truth that sets them free.

And we, who know how true Thou art,
 And Thee as God and Lord adore,
Give us, we pray, a loyal heart,
 To trust and love Thee more and more.

W. Bright.

77.

WHILE shepherds watched their flocks by night,
   All seated on the ground,
The angel of the Lord came down,
   And glory shone around.

"Fear not," said he ; for mighty dread
   Had seized their troubled mind ;
'Glad tidings of great joy I bring
   To you and all mankind.

"To you in David's town this day
   Is born of David's line
A Saviour, Who is Christ the Lord ;
   And this shall be the sign :

"The heavenly Babe you there shall find
   To human view displayed,
All meanly wrapped in swathing bands,
   And in a manger laid."

Thus spake the seraph, and forthwith
   Appeared a shining throng
Of angels praising God, who thus
   Addressed their joyful song :

"All Glory be to God on high,
   And on the earth be peace ;
Goodwill henceforth from heaven to men
   Begin and never cease !"

N. Tate.

78.

HARK! the herald-angels sing
   Glory to the new-born King,
Peace on earth and mercy mild,
God and sinners reconciled.
Joyful, all ye nations, rise,
Join the triumph of the skies;
With the angelic host proclaim,
" Christ is born in Bethlehem!"
     Hark! the herald-angels sing
     Glory to the new-born King.

Christ, by highest Heaven adored,
Christ, the everlasting Lord,
Late in time behold him come,
Offspring of a Virgin's womb.
Veiled in flesh the Godhead see;
Hail! the Incarnate Deity!
Man with man He deigns to dwell,
Jesus, our Immanuel.
     Hark! the herald-angels sing
     Glory to the new-born King.

Hail! the heaven-born Prince of Peace!
Hail! the Sun of Righteousness!
Light and life to all He brings,
Risen with healing in His wings.
Mild He lays His glory by,
Born that man no more may die,
Born to raise the sons of earth,
Born to give them second birth.
     Hark! the herald-angels sing
     Glory to the new-born King.

C. Wesley.

79.

IN the field with their flocks abiding,
  They lay on the dewy ground ;
And glimmering under the starlight
  The sheep lay white around ;
When the light of the Lord streamed o'er them,
  And lo ! from the heaven above
An angel leaned from the glory,
  And sang his song of love :
    He sang, that first sweet Christmas,
      The song that shall never cease :
    "Glory to God in the highest,
      On earth good-will and peace !"

"To you in the city of David
  A Saviour is born to-day."
And sudden a host of the heavenly ones
  Flashed forth to join the lay.
Oh ! never hath sweeter message
  Thrilled home to the souls of men,
And the heavens themselves had never heard
  A gladder choir till then :
    For they sang that Christmas carol
      That never on earth shall cease :
    "Glory to God in the highest,
      On earth good-will and peace !"

And the shepherds came to the manger,
  And gazed on the Holy Child,
And calmly o'er that rude cradle
  The Virgin Mother smiled ;
And the sky, in the starlight silence,
  Seemed full of the angel lay :
"To you in the city of David
  A Saviour is born to-day."
    Oh ! they sang—and I ween that never
      The carol on earth shall cease—
    "Glory to God in the highest,
      On earth good-will and peace !"

F. W. Farrar.

80.

ANGELS, from the realms of glory,
  Wing your flight o'er all the earth ;
Ye who sang Creation's story,
  Now proclaim Messiah's birth ;
    Come and worship,
  Worship Christ the new-born King.

Shepherds, in the field abiding,
  Watching o'er your flocks by night,
God with man is now residing,
  Round you shines the heavenly light ;
    Come and worship,
  Worship Christ the new-born King.

Saints, before the altar bending,
  Watching long in hope and fear,
Suddenly the Lord, descending,
  In His temple shall appear ;
    Come and worship,
  Worship Christ the new-born King.

J. Montgomery.

81.

A DESTE, fideles,
  Læti triumphantes;
Venite, venite in Bethlehem;
  Natum videte
  Regem angelorum:
Venite adoremus Dominum.

  Deum de Deo,
  Lumen de Lumine,
Gestant puellæ viscera
  Deum Verum,
  Genitum non factum:
Venite adoremus Dominum.

  Cantet nunc hymnos
  Chorus angelorum,
Cantet nunc aula cælestium,
  "Gloria
  In excelsis Deo!"
Venite adoremus Dominum.

  Ergo Qui natus
  Die hodierna,
Jesu, Tibi sit gloria;
  Patris Aeterni
  Verbum Caro factum:
Venite adoremus Dominum.

82.

O COME, all ye faithful,
    Joyful and triumphant,
O come ye, O come ye, to Bethlehem.
    Come and behold Him,
    Born the King of angels ;
    O come, let us adore Him,
    O come, let us adore Him,
O come, let us adore Him, Christ the Lord !

    God of God,
    Light of Light,
Lo ! He abhors not the Virgin's womb ;
    Very God,
    Begotten, not created ;
O come, let us adore Him, Christ the Lord !

    Sing, choirs of angels,
    Sing in exultation,
Sing, all ye citizens of heaven above,
    " Glory to God
    In the highest ":
O come, let us adore Him, Christ the Lord !

    Yea, Lord, we greet Thee,
    Born this happy morning ;
Jesus, to Thee be glory given,
    Word of the Father,
    Now in flesh appearing ;
O come, let us adore Him, Christ the Lord !

F. Oakeley.

83.

CHRISTIANS, awake ! salute the happy morn,
  Whereon the Saviour of the world was born ;
Rise to adore the mystery of love
Which hosts of angels chanted from above :
With them the joyful tidings first begun
Of God Incarnate and the Virgin's Son.

Then to the watchful shepherds it was told,
Who heard the angelic herald's voice, " Behold,
I bring good tidings of a Saviour's birth
To you and all the nations upon earth :
This day hath God fulfilled His promised Word,
This day is born a Saviour, Christ the Lord."

He spake ; and straightway the celestial choir
In hymns of joy, unknown before, conspire :
The praises of redeeming love they sang,
And heaven's whole orb with Alleluias rang :
God's highest glory was their anthem still,
Peace upon earth, and unto men good will.

To Bethlehem straight the enlightened shepherds ran,
To see the wonder God had wrought for man,
And found, with Joseph and the blessèd Maid,
Her Son, the Saviour, in a manger laid :
Then to their flocks, still praising God, return,
And their glad hearts with holy rapture burn.

Oh ! may we keep and ponder in our mind
God's wondrous love in saving lost mankind ;
Trace we the Babe, Who hath retrieved our loss,
From the poor manger to the bitter Cross ;
Tread in His steps, through lowly toil and pain,
Till man's first heavenly state be ours again.

Then may we hope, the angelic hosts among,
To sing, redeemed, a glad triumphal song :
He that was born upon this joyful day
Around us all His glory shall display ;
Saved by His love, incessant we shall sing
Eternal praise to heaven's Almighty King.

J. Byrom.

84.

I SING the birth was born to-night,
  The Author both of life and light,
The angels so did sound it ;
And like the ravished shepherds said,
Who saw the light and were afraid,
  Yet searched, and true they found it.

The Son of God, th' Eternal King,
That did us all salvation bring,
  And freed the soul from danger ;
He, Whom the whole world could not take,
The Word which heaven and earth did make,
  Was now laid in a manger.

The Father's wisdom willed it so,
The Son's obedience knew no No,
  Both wills were in one stature :
And as that wisdom had decreed,
The Word was now made flesh indeed,
  And took on Him our nature.

What comfort by Him do we win,
Who made Himself the price of sin
  To make us heirs of glory !
To see this Babe all innocence,
A martyr born in our defence —
  Can man forget this story ?

Ben. Jonson.

85.

I T came upon the midnight clear,
   That glorious song of old,
From angels bending near the earth
   To touch their harps of gold,
" Peace to the earth, good will to men "
   From heaven's all gracious King :
The world in solemn stillness lay
   To hear the angels sing.

Still through the cloven skies they come
   With peaceful wings unfurled ;
And still their heavenly music floats
   O'er all the weary world :
Above its sad and lowly plains
   They bend on hovering wing,
And ever o'er its Babel sounds
   The blessèd angels sing.

And ye, beneath life's crushing load
   Whose forms are bending low,
Who toil along the climbing way
   With painful steps and slow ;
Look now, for glad and golden hours
   Come swiftly on the wing :
Oh ! rest beside the weary road,
   And hear the angels sing.

For lo ! the days are hastening on,
   By prophet-bards foretold,
When with the ever-circling years
   Comes round the age of gold ;
When Peace shall over all the earth
   Its ancient splendour fling,
And the whole world send back the song
   Which now the angels sing.

E. H. Sears.

86.

ALL my heart this night rejoices,
    As I hear,
    Far and near,
Sweetest angel voices ;
" Christ is born ! " their choirs are singing,
    Till the air
    Everywhere
Now with joy is ringing.

Hark ! a voice from yonder manger,
    Soft and sweet,
    Doth entreat,
" Flee from woe and danger ;
Brethren, come ! from all doth grieve you
    You are freed ;
    All you need
I will surely give you."

Come, then, let us hasten yonder ;
    Here let all,
    Great and small,
Kneel in awe and wonder ;
Love Him Who with love is yearning ;
    Hail the star
    That from far
Bright with hope is burning.

C. Winkworth.
(*Translation from the German
of P. Gerhardt*).

87.

FIRST of martyrs, thou whose name
    Doth thy golden crown proclaim,
Not of flowers that fade away
Weave we this thy crown to-day.

Bright the stones which bruise thee gleam,
Sprinkled with thy life-blood's stream ;
Stars around thy sainted head
Never could such radiance shed.

Every wound upon thy brow
Sparkles with unearthly glow ;
Like an angel's is thy face
Beaming with celestial grace.

Oh ! how blessèd first to be
Slain for Him Who bled for thee ;
First like Him in dying hour
Witness to Almighty power !

Glory to the Father be,
Glory, Virgin-born, to Thee,
Glory to the Holy Ghost,
Praised by men and heavenly host !

Translation from the Latin of J. B. de Santeuil.

88.

" LORD, and what shall this man do?"
    Ask'st thou, Christian, for thy friend?
If his love for Christ be true,
    Christ hath told thee of his end:
This is he whom God approves,
This is he whom Jesus loves.

Ask not of him more than this;
    Leave it in his Saviour's breast,
Whether, early called to bliss,
    He in youth shall find his rest,
Or armèd in his station wait
Till his Lord be at the gate.

Sick or healthful, slave or free,
    Wealthy or despised and poor—
What is that to him or thee,
    So his love to Christ endure?
When the shore is won at last,
Who will count the billows past?

J. Keble.

89.

O HOLY Lord, content to dwell
  In a poor home, a lowly Child,
With meek obedience noting well
  Each bidding of Thy Mother mild ;

Lead every child that bears Thy Name
  To walk in Thy pure upright way,
To dread the touch of sin and shame,
  And humbly, like Thyself, obey.

Oh ! let not this world's scorching glow
  Thy Spirit's quickening dew efface,
Nor blast of sin too rudely blow,
  And quench the trembling flame of grace.

Gather Thy lambs within Thine arm,
  And gently in Thy bosom bear ;
Keep them, O Lord, from hurt and harm,
  And bid them rest for ever there.

So shall they, waiting here below
  Like Thee, their Lord, a little span,
In wisdom and in stature grow,
  And favour both with God and man.

Bishop Walsham How.

90.

TO the Name of our salvation
  Laud and honour let us pay,
Which for many a generation
  Hid in God's foreknowledge lay,
But with holy exultation
  We may sing aloud to-day.

Jesus is the Name we treasure,
  Name beyond what words can tell ;
Name of gladness, Name of pleasure,
  Ear and heart delighting well ;
Name of sweetness passing measure,
  Saving us from sin and hell.

'Tis the Name for adoration,
  Name for songs of victory,
Name for holy meditation
  In this vale of misery,
Name for joyful veneration
  By the citizens on high.

'Tis the Name that whoso preacheth
  Speaks like music to the ear ;
Who in prayer this Name beseecheth
  Sweetest comfort findeth near ;
Who its perfect wisdom reacheth
  Heavenly joy possesseth here.

Jesus is the Name exalted
  Over every other name ;
In this Name, whene'er assaulted,
  We can put our foes to shame ;
Strength to them who else had halted,
  Eyes to blind, and feet to lame.

Therefore we in love adoring
  This most blessèd Name revere,
Holy Jesu, Thee imploring
  So to write it in us here,
That hereafter heavenward soaring
  We may sing with angels there.

J. M. Neale.
(*Translation from the Latin*).

91.

EARTH has many a noble city ;
  Bethlehem, thou dost all excel :
Out of thee the Lord from heaven
  Came to rule His Israel.

Fairer than the sun at morning
  Was the star that told His birth,
To the world its God announcing
  Seen in fleshly form on earth.

Eastern sages at His cradle
  Make oblations rich and rare ;
See them give, in deep devotion,
  Gold and frankincense and myrrh ;

Sacred gifts of mystic meaning :
  Incense doth their God disclose,
Gold the King of kings proclaimeth,
  Myrrh His sepulchre foreshows.

Jesu, whom the Gentiles worshipped
  At Thy glad Epiphany,
Unto Thee, with God the Father
  And the Spirit, glory be !

E. Caswall.
(Translation from the Latin
of Prudentius)

92.

BRIGHTEST and best of the sons of the morning,
    Dawn on our darkness and lend us thine aid ;
Star of the East, the horizon adorning,
    Guide where our Infant Redeemer is laid.

Cold on His cradle the dew-drops are shining,
    Low lies His head with the beasts of the stall ;
Angels adore Him in slumber reclining,
    Maker and Monarch and Saviour of all.

Say, shall we yield Him, in costly devotion,
    Odours of Edom and offerings divine ?
Gems of the mountain and pearls of the ocean,
    Myrrh from the forest or gold from the mine ?

Vainly we offer each ample oblation,
    Vainly with gifts would His favour secure ;
Richer by far is the heart's adoration,
    Dearer to God are the prayers of the poor.

Brightest and best of the sons of the morning,
    Dawn on our darkness and lend us thine aid ;
Star of the East, the horizon adorning,
    Guide where our Infant Redeemer is laid.

Bishop Heber.

93.

BLEST are the pure in heart,
For they shall see our God;
The secret of the Lord is theirs,
Their soul is Christ's abode.

The Lord, Who left the heavens
Our life and peace to bring,
To dwell in lowliness with men,
Their Pattern and their King;

He to the lowly soul
Doth still Himself impart,
And for His cradle and His throne
Chooseth the pure in heart.

Lord, we Thy presence seek;
May ours this blessing be;
Give us a pure and lowly heart,
A temple meet for Thee.

J. Keble.

94.

FROM the eastern mountains
    Pressing on they come,
Wise men in their wisdom,
    To His humble home ;
Stirred by deep devotion,
    Hastening from afar,
Ever journeying onward,
    Guided by a star.

There their Lord and Saviour
    Meek and lowly lay :
Wondrous light that led them
    Onward on their way,
Evermore to lighten
    Nations from afar,
As they journey homeward
    By that guiding star!

Thou, Who in a manger
    Once hast lowly lain,
Who dost now in glory
    O'er all kingdoms reign,
Gather in the heathen,
    Who in lands afar
Ne'er have seen the brightness
    Of Thy guiding star ;

Until every nation,
    Whether bond or free,
'Neath Thy starlit banner,
    Jesu, follows Thee
O'er the distant mountains
    To that heavenly home,
Where nor sin nor sorrow
    Evermore shall come.

G. Thring.

95.

HOW brightly beams the morning star !
What sudden radiance from afar
Doth glad us with its shining !
Brightness of God, that breaks our night
And fills the darkened souls with light
Who long for truth were pining !
Thy word, Jesu,
Inly feeds us,
Rightly leads us,
Life bestowing :
Praise, oh ! praise such love o'erflowing !

Thou here my Comfort, there my Crown,
Thou King of heaven, Who camest down
To dwell as man beside me,
My heart doth praise Thee o'er and o'er ;
If Thou art mine, I ask no more,
Be wealth or fame denied me :
Thee I seek now ;
None who proves Thee,
None who loves Thee
Finds Thee fail him :
Lord of Life, Thy powers avail him.

Oh ! praise to Him Who came to save,
Who conquered death and burst the grave !
Each day new praise resoundeth
To Him the Lamb Who once was slain,
The Friend Whom none shall trust in vain,
Whose grace for aye aboundeth.
Sing, ye heavens,
Tell the story
Of His glory,
Till His praises
Flood with light earth's darkest places !

C. Winkworth.
(*Translation from the German
of J. A. Schlegel*).

96.

AS with gladness men of old
  Did the guiding star behold ;
As with joy they hailed its light,
Leading onward, beaming bright ;
So, most gracious Lord, may we
Evermore be led to Thee.

As with joyful steps they sped
To that lowly manger-bed,
There to bend the knee before
Him Whom Heaven and Earth adore ;
So may we with willing feet
Ever seek Thy mercy-seat.

As they offered gifts most rare
At that manger rude and bare ;
So may we with holy joy,
Pure and free from sin's alloy,
All our costliest treasures bring,
Christ, to Thee our heavenly King.

Holy Jesus, every day
Keep us in the narrow way ;
And, when earthly things are past
Bring our ransomed souls at last
Where they need no star to guide,
Where no clouds Thy glory hide.

W. C. Dix.

97.

HAIL to the Lord's Anointed,
　Great David's greater Son !
Hail, in the time appointed,
　His reign on earth begun !
He comes to break oppression,
　To set the captive free,
To take away transgression,
　And rule in equity.

Kings shall fall down before Him
　And gold and incense bring ;
All nations shall adore Him,
　His praise all people sing ;
For He shall have dominion
　O'er river, sea, and shore,
Far as the eagle's pinion
　Or dove's light wing can soar.

To Him shall prayer unceasing
　And daily vows ascend,
His kingdom still increasing,
　A kingdom without end :
The mountain dews shall nourish
　A seed, in weakness sown,
Whose fruit shall spread and flourish,
　And shake like Lebanon.

O'er every foe victorious
　He on His throne shall rest,
From age to age more glorious,
　All-blessing and all-blessed :
The tide of time shall never
　His covenant remove ;
His Name shall stand for ever,
　His great, best Name of Love.

J. Montgomery.

98.

OH! worship the King all glorious above!
  Oh! gratefully sing His power and His love!
Our Shield and Defender, the Ancient of Days,
Pavilioned with splendour and girded with praise!

Oh! tell of His might, oh! sing of His grace,
Whose robe is the light, whose canopy space:
His chariots of wrath the deep thunder-clouds form,
And dark is His path on the wings of the storm.

This earth, with its stores of wonders untold,
Almighty, Thy power hath founded of old;
Hath stablished it fast by a changeless decree,
And round it hath cast like a mantle the sea.

Thy bountiful care what tongue can recite?
It breathes in the air, it shines in the light,
It streams from the hills, it descends to the plain,
And sweetly distils in the dew and the rain.

Frail children of dust, and feeble as frail,
In Thee do we trust, nor find Thee to fail:
Thy mercies how tender, how sure to the end,
Our Maker, Defender, Redeemer and Friend!

Sir R. Grant.

99.

I PRAISED the earth, in beauty seen
  With garlands gay of various green ;
I praised the sea, whose ample field
Shone glorious as a silver shield ;
And earth and ocean seemed to say,
"Our beauties are but for a day."

I praised the sun, whose chariot rolled
On wheels of amber and of gold ;
I praised the moon, whose softer eye
Gleamed sweetly through the summer sky ;
And moon and sun in answer said,
"Our days of light are numberèd."

O God, O Good beyond compare,
If thus Thy meaner works are fair,
If thus Thy bounties gild the span
Of ruined earth and sinful man,
How glorious must the mansions be
Where Thy redeemed shall dwell with Thee !

Bishop Heber.

100.

Y E boundless realms of joy,
  Exalt your Maker's fame,
His praise your song employ
  Above the starry frame !
    Your voices raise,
      Ye Cherubim
      And Seraphim,
    To sing His praise !

Thou moon, that rul'st the night,
  And sun, that guid'st the day,
Ye glittering stars of light,
  To Him your homage pay !
    His praise declare,
      Ye heavens above,
      And clouds that move
    In liquid air !

Let them adore the Lord,
  And praise His holy Name,
By Whose Almighty Word
  They all from nothing came :
    And all shall last
      From changes free ;
      His firm decree
    Stands ever fast.

N. Tate and N. Brady.

101.

THE strain upraise of joy and praise,   Alleluia!

To the glory of their King
Shall the ransomed people sing   Alleluia!

And the choirs that dwell on high
Shall re-echo through the sky   Alleluia!

They through the fields of Paradise who roam,
The blessed ones, repeat through that bright home
                                        Alleluia!

The planets, beaming on their heavenly way,
The shining constellations join, and say   Alleluia!

Ye clouds that onward sweep,
    Ye winds on pinions light,
Ye thunders, echoing loud and deep,
    Ye lightnings, wildly bright,
In sweet consent unite your   Alleluia!

Ye floods and ocean billows,
    Ye storms and winter snow,
Ye days of cloudless beauty,
    Hoar frost, and summer glow,
Ye groves that wave in spring,
And glorious forests, sing   Alleluia!

First let the birds, with painted plumage gay,
Exalt their great Creator's praise, and say
                                        Alleluia!

Then let the beasts of earth, with varying strain,
Join in Creation's hymn, and cry again   Alleluia !

Here let the mountains thunder forth sonorous
                                                    Alleluia !
There let the valleys sing in gentler chorus Alleluia !

Thou jubilant abyss of ocean, cry   Alleluia !

Ye tracts of earth and continents, reply   Alleluia !

    To God, Who all Creation made,
    The frequent hymn be duly paid ;   Alleluia !

This is the strain, the eternal strain, the Lord
    Almighty loves ;   Alleluia !
This is the song, the heavenly song, that Christ
    Himself approves :   Alleluia !

Wherefore we sing, both heart and voice awaking,
                                                    Alleluia !
And children's voices echo, answer making,
                                                    Alleluia !

    Now from all men be outpoured
    Alleluia to the Lord ;
    With Alleluia evermore
    The Son and Spirit we adore.

Praise be done to the Three in One !
    Alleluia !   Alleluia !   Alleluia !

J. M. Neale.
(Translation from the Latin).

102.

THE spacious firmament on high,
　　With all the blue ethereal sky,
And spangled heavens, a shining frame
Their great Original proclaim.
The unwearied sun from day to day
Does his Creator's power display,
And publishes to every land
The work of an Almighty Hand.

Soon as the evening shades prevail,
The moon takes up the wondrous tale,
And nightly to the listening earth
Repeats the story of her birth ;
Whilst all the stars that round her burn,
And all the planets in their turn,
Confirm the tidings as they roll,
And spread the truth from pole to pole.

What though in solemn silence all
Move round the dark terrestrial ball?
What though nor real voice nor sound
Amid their radiant orbs be found?
In reason's ear they all rejoice,
And utter forth a glorious voice,
For ever singing, as they shine,
"The Hand that made us is divine."

J. Addison.

103.

FOR the beauty of the earth,
    For the glory of the skies,
For the love which from our birth
    Over and around us lies,
        Lord of all, to Thee we raise
        This our grateful psalm of praise.

For the wonder of each hour
    Of the day and of the night,
Hill and vale, and tree and flower,
    Sun and moon, and stars of light,
        Lord of all, to Thee we raise
        This our grateful psalm of praise.

For the joy of human love,
    Brother, sister, parent, child,
Friends on earth, and friends above,
    Pleasures pure and undefiled,
        Lord of all, to Thee we raise
        This our grateful psalm of praise.

For Thy Church that evermore
    Lifteth holy hands above,
Offering up on every shore
    Her pure sacrifice of love,
        Lord of all, to Thee we raise
        This our grateful psalm of praise.

F. S. Pierpoint.

104.

THERE is a book, who runs may read,
  Which heavenly truth imparts ;
And all the lore its scholars need,
  Pure eyes and Christian hearts.

The works of God above, below,
  Within us and around,
Are pages in that book to show
  How God Himself is found.

The glorious sky embracing all
  Is like the Maker's love,
Wherewith encompassed, great and small
  In peace and order move.

The moon above, the Church below,
  A wondrous race they run ;
But all their radiance, all their glow,
  Each borrows of its Sun.

Two worlds are ours : 'tis only sin
  Forbids us to descry
The mystic heaven and earth within,
  Plain as the sea and sky.

Thou, Who hast given me eyes to see
  And love this sight so fair,
Give me a heart to find out Thee,
  And read Thee everywhere.

                              J. Keble.

105.

JERUSALEM, my happy home,
  Name ever dear to me,
When shall my labours have an end
  In joy and peace and thee?

When shall these eyes thy heaven-built walls
  And gates of pearl behold,
Thy bulwarks with salvation strong,
  And streets of shining gold?

Apostles, martyrs, prophets, there
  Around my Saviour stand;
And all I love in Christ below
  Shall join that glorious band.

Jerusalem, my happy home,
  My souls still longs for thee;
Then shall my labours have an end,
  When I thy joys shall see.

Ascribed to F. Baker.

106.

JERUSALEM the golden,
　With milk and honey blest ;
Beneath thy contemplation
　Sink heart and voice oppressed.
I know not, oh ! I know not
　What joys await us there,
What radiancy of glory,
　What bliss beyond compare.

They stand, those halls of Sion,
　All jubilant with song,
And bright with many an angel,
　And all the martyr throng :
The Prince is ever in them,
　The daylight is serene ;
The pastures of the blessèd
　Are decked in glorious sheen.

There is the throne of David ;
　And there, from care released,
The shout of them that triumph,
　The song of them that feast ;
And they, who with their Leader
　Have conquered in the fight,
For ever and for ever
　Are clad in robes of white.

J. M. Neale.
(*Translation from the Latin
of Bernard of Morlaix*).

107.

PRAISE to the Holiest in the height,
  And in the depth be praise ;
In all His words most wonderful,
  Most sure in all His ways !

O loving wisdom of our God !
  When all was sin and shame,
A second Adam to the fight
  And to the rescue came.

O wisest love ! that flesh and blood,
  Which did in Adam fail,
Should strive afresh against the foe,
  Should strive and should prevail ;

And that a higher gift than grace
  Should flesh and blood refine,
God's Presence and His very Self,
  And Essence all-divine.

O generous love ! that He, Who smote
  In man for man the foe,
The double agony in man
  For man should undergo ;

And in the garden secretly,
  And on the Cross on high,
Should teach His brethren and inspire
  To suffer and to die.

Praise to the Holiest in the height
  And in the depth be praise ;
In all His words most wonderful,
  Most sure in all His ways !

Cardinal Newman.

108.

LORD Jesus, are we one with Thee?
　　O height, O depth of love!
Thou one with us on Calvary,
　We one with Thee above!

Such was Thy love, that for our sake
　Thou didst from Heaven come down;
Our mortal flesh and blood partake,
　In all our misery one.

Our sins, our guilt, in love divine,
　Confessed and borne by Thee!
The sting, the curse, the wrath, were Thine,
　To set Thy members free.

Ascended now, in glory bright,
　Still one with us Thou art;
Nor life, nor death, nor depth, nor height
　Thy saints and Thee can part.

Ere long shall come that glorious Day
　When, seated on Thy throne,
Thou shalt to wondering worlds display
　That we in Thee are one.

J. G. Deck.

109.

GRACIOUS Spirit, Holy Ghost,
  Taught by Thee, we covet most
Of Thy gifts at Pentecost
  Holy, heavenly Love.

Faith, that mountains could remove,
Tongues of earth or heaven above,
Knowledge, all things, empty prove,
  Without heavenly Love.

Love is kind, and suffers long,
Love is meek, and thinks no wrong,
Love than death itself more strong ;
  Therefore give us Love.

Prophecy will fade away,
Melting in the light of day ;
Love will ever with us stay ;
  Therefore give us Love.

Faith will vanish into sight ;
Hope be emptied in delight ;
Love in heaven will shine more bright ;
  Therefore give us Love.

Faith and Hope and Love we see
Joining hand in hand agree ;
But the greatest of the three,
  And the best, is Love.

Bishop Christopher Wordsworth.

110.

LORD of Love, Whose words have taught us
How to serve Thee and obey ;
Lord of Love, Whose deeds have brought us
Wondering at Thy feet to pray ;
Fill our hearts with ample measure
Of the Christian graces three ;
Most of all with Thy dear treasure,
Never-failing Charity ;

Charity, that ever bindeth
Mortal men with cords of love ;
Charity, that still remindeth
Earthly souls of heaven above ;
Charity, the Spirit's token,
Sinners have received of Thee :
He whom Jesus loved hath spoken,
God Himself is Charity.

J. Sedgwick.

111.

O LORD, turn not Thy face away
   From them that lowly lie,
Lamenting sore their sinful life
   With tears and bitter cry.
Thy mercy-gates are open wide
   To them that mourn their sin ;
Oh ! shut them not against us, Lord,
   But let us enter in.

We need not to confess our faults,
   For surely Thou canst tell ;
What we have done, and what we are,
   Thou knowest very well :
Therefore, to beg and to entreat,
   With tears we come to Thee,
As children that have done amiss,
   Fall at their father's knee.

And need we then, O Lord, repeat
   The blessing which we crave,
When Thou dost know, before we speak
   The thing that we would have?
Mercy, O Lord, mercy we seek ;
   This is the total sum :
For mercy, Lord, is all our prayer ;
   Oh ! let Thy mercy come.

J. Marckant and Bishop Heber.

112.

JUST as I am, without one plea,
　But that Thy blood was shed for me,
And that Thou bidd'st me come to Thee,
　　　　　O Lamb of God, I come.

Just as I am, and waiting not
To rid my soul of one dark blot,
To Thee, Whose blood can cleanse each spot,
　　　　　O Lamb of God, I come.

Just as I am, though tossed about
With many a conflict, many a doubt,
Fightings and fears, within, without,
　　　　　O Lamb of God, I come.

Just as I am, poor, wretched, blind,
Sight, riches, healing of the mind,
Yea, all I need, in Thee to find,
　　　　　O Lamb of God, I come.

Just as I am—Thou wilt receive,
Wilt welcome, pardon, cleanse, relieve,
Because Thy promise I believe—
　　　　　O Lamb of God, I come.

Just as I am—Thy love unknown
Has broken every barrier down—
Now to be Thine, yea, Thine alone,
　　　　　O Lamb of God, I come.

Just as I am, of that free love
The breadth, length, depth, and height to prove
Here for a season, then above,
　　　　　O Lamb of God, I come.

C. Elliott.

113.

OH ! help us, Lord ; each hour of need
　　Thy heavenly succour give,
Help us in thought, and word, and deed,
　　Each hour on earth we live.

Oh ! help us when our spirits bleed
　　With contrite anguish sore ;
And when our hearts are cold and dead,
　　Oh ! help us, Lord, the more.

Oh ! help us, through the prayer of faith
　　More firmly to believe ;
For still the more the servant hath,
　　The more shall he receive.

Oh ! help us, Saviour, from on high ;
　　We know no help but Thee :
Oh ! help us so to live and die
　　As Thine in heaven to be.

Dean Milman.

114.

SAVIOUR, when in dust to Thee
Low we bow the adoring knee,
When, repentant, to the skies
Scarce we lift our weeping eyes,
Oh ! by all the pains and woe
Suffered once for man below,
Bending from Thy throne on high,
Hear our solemn litany !

By Thy helpless infant years,
By Thy life of want and tears,
By Thy days of sore distress
In the savage wilderness,
By the dread mysterious hour
Of the insulting tempter's power,
Turn, oh ! turn a favouring eye,
Hear our solemn litany !

By the sacred griefs that wept
O'er the grave where Lazarus slept,
By the boding tears that flowed
Over Salem's loved abode,
By the anguished sigh that told
Treachery lurked within Thy fold,
From Thy seat above the sky
Hear our solemn litany !

By Thine hour of dire despair,
By Thine agony and prayer,
By the Cross, the nail, the thorn,
Piercing spear, and torturing scorn,
By the gloom that veiled the skies
O'er the dreadful sacrifice,
Listen to our humble cry,
Hear our solemn litany !

By Thy deep expiring groan,
By the sad sepulchral stone,
By the vault whose dark abode
Held in vain the rising God,
Oh! from earth to heaven restored,
Mighty re-ascended Lord,
Listen, listen to the cry
Of our solemn litany!

Sir R. Grant.

115.

L ORD, in this Thy mercy's day,
　Ere it pass for aye away,
On our knees we fall and pray.

Holy Jesus, grant us tears,
Fill us with heart-searching fears,
Ere that awful doom appears.

Lord, on us Thy Spirit pour,
Kneeling lowly at the door,
Ere it close for evermore.

By Thy night of agony,
By Thy supplicating cry,
By Thy willingness to die,

By Thy tears of bitter woe
For Jerusalem below,
Let us not Thy love forego.

Grant us 'neath Thy wings a place,
Lest we lose this day of grace,
Ere we shall behold Thy face.

I. Williams.

116.

SAVIOUR, when temptations try us,
  And our strength is like to fail,
May the thought that Thou art by us
  Lend us courage to prevail.

If the foe has dared to enter,
  Fought, and turned at last to flee,
Take away our pride, and centre
  All our gratitude on Thee.

If the conflict overtake us,
  And we fight and fail to win,
Banish blind despair, and make us
  Braver in the war with sin.

Should we e'er in mean submission
  Basely yield without a blow,
May the tears of true contrition
  Testify our shame and woe.

Saviour, Thou hast known temptation,
  Thou hast felt its deadly power ;
Succour us with Thy salvation,
  Aid us in the evil hour.

E. W. Howson.

117.

NOT in anger, mighty God,
　　Not in anger smite us ;
We must perish if Thy rod
　Justly should requite us :
　　We are nought ;
　　Sin hath brought,
　Lord, Thy wrath upon us ;
　Yet have mercy on us.

Show me now a Father's love,
　And His tender patience ;
Heal my wounded soul, remove
　These too sore temptations :
　　I am weak ;
　　Father, speak
　Thou of peace and gladness ;
　Comfort Thou my sadness.

Father, hymns to Thee we raise,
　Here and soon in heaven ;
And the Son and Spirit praise
　Who our bonds have riven :
　　Evermore
　　We adore
　Thee, Whose grace hath stirred us,
　And Whose pity heard us.

C. Winkworth.
*(Translation from the German
of J. G. Albinus).*

118.

B LOT out our sins of old,
    When erst we went astray,
When, Father, from Thy fold
    We wandered far away :
        O King of Heaven,
            To Thee we cry,
            Ere yet we die,
        To be forgiven.

In this our hour of need,
    In hope we fly to Thee ;
Sow in our hearts the seed
    Of bright eternity :
        O Lord, we pray,
            As morning dew
            Our strength renew
        From day to day.

O God, by day, by night,
    We lowly bend the knee ;
Again at dawn of light,
    In deep humility,
        Our voices raise
            For sins forgiven,
            And hopes of heaven,
        In prayer and praise.

Blot out our sins gone by,
    Blot out our sins to-day,
And others ere we die ;
    And give us, while we pray,
        Undying faith
            In Christ, to see
            The victory
        O'er sin and death.

G. Thring.

2/10/07

119.

ROCK of Ages, cleft for me,
    Let me hide myself in Thee ;
Let the water and the blood,
From Thy riven side which flowed,
Be of sin the double cure,
Cleanse me from its guilt and power.

Not the labours of my hands
Can fulfil Thy law's demands ;
Could my zeal no respite know,
Could my tears for ever flow,
All for sin could not atone ;
Thou must save, and Thou alone.

Nothing in my hand I bring,
Simply to Thy Cross I cling :
Naked come to Thee for dress ;
Helpless, look to Thee for grace ;
Foul, I to the Fountain fly ;
Wash me, Saviour, or I die.

While I draw this fleeting breath,
When my eyelids close in death,
When I soar through tracts unknown,
See Thee on Thy judgment throne,
Rock of Ages, cleft for me,
Let me hide myself in Thee.

A. M. Toplady.

120.

IN the hour of trial,
  Jesu, pray for me ;
Lest by base denial
  I depart from Thee :
When Thou seest me waver,
  With a look recall,
Nor for fear or favour
  Suffer me to fall.

With its witching pleasures
  Would this vain world charm,
Or its sordid treasures
  Spread to work me harm,
Bring to my remembrance
  Sad Gethsemane
Or in darker semblance
  Cross-crowned Calvary.

If with sore affliction
  Thou in love chastise,
Pour Thy benediction
  On the sacrifice :
Then, upon Thine altar
  Freely offered up,
Though the flesh may falter,
  Faith shall drink the cup.

When in dust and ashes
  To the grave I sink,
While heaven's glory flashes
  O'er the shelving brink,
On Thy truth relying
  Through that mortal strife,
Lord, receive me dying
  To eternal life.

J. Montgomery.

121.

WHEN our heads are bowed with woe,
  When our bitter tears o'erflow,
When we mourn the lost, the dear,
Jesu, Son of Mary, hear.

Thou our throbbing flesh hast worn,
Thou our mortal griefs hast borne,
Thou hast shed the human tear ;
Jesu, Son of Mary, hear.

When the sullen death-bell tolls
For our own departed souls ;
When our final doom is near,
Jesu, Son of Mary, hear.

Thou hast bowed the dying head,
Thou the blood of life hast shed,
Thou hast filled a mortal bier ;
Jesu, Son of Mary, hear.

When the heart is sad within
With the sense of all its sin ;
When the spirit shrinks with fear,
Jesu, Son of Mary, hear.

Thou the shame, the grief hast known,
Though the sins were not Thine own ;
Thou hast deigned their load to bear ;
Jesu, Son of Mary, hear.

Dean Milman.

122.

WHY should I fear the darkest hour,
  Or tremble at the tempter's power?
Jesus vouchsafes to be my Tower.

Though hot the fight, why quit the field?
Why must I either fly or yield,
Since Jesus is my mighty Shield?

I know not what may soon betide,
Or how my wants shall be supplied;
But Jesus knows, and will provide.

Though sin would fill me with distress,
The throne of grace I dare address,
For Jesus is my Righteousness.

Though faint my prayers, and cold my love,
My steadfast hope shall not remove,
While Jesus intercedes above.

Against me earth and hell combine;
But on my side is power divine;
Jesus is All, and He is mine.

J. Newton.

123.

IN the hour of my distress,
　When temptations me oppress,
And when I my sins confess,
　Sweet Spirit, comfort me.

When I lie upon my bed
Sick in heart and sick in head,
And with doubts discomforted,
　Sweet Spirit, comfort me.

When the house doth sigh and weep,
And the world is drowned in sleep,
While mine eyes their night-watch keep,
　Sweet Spirit, comfort me.

When the tempter me pursueth,
And the sins of all my youth
Stand arrayed in naked truth,
　Sweet Spirit, comfort me.

When the Judgment is revealed,
And the book of doom unsealed,
When to Thee I have appealed,
　Sweet Spirit, comfort me.

R. Herrick.

124

WHEN gathering clouds around I view,
And days are dark, and friends are few,
On Him I lean Who not in vain
Experienced every human pain ;
He sees my wants, allays my fears,
And counts and treasures up my tears.

If aught should tempt my soul to stray
From heavenly wisdom's narrow way,
To flee the good I would pursue,
Or do the sin I would not do,
Still He, Who felt temptation's power,
Shall guard me in that dangerous hour.

When vexing thoughts within me rise,
And sore dismayed my spirit dies,
Yet He, Who once vouchsafed to bear
The sickening anguish of despair,
Shall sweetly soothe, shall gently dry,
The throbbing heart, the streaming eye.

When sorrowing o'er some stone I bend
Which covers all that was a friend,
And from his hand, his voice, his smile,
Divides me for a little while ;
Thou, Saviour, mark'st the tears I shed,
For Thou didst weep o'er Lazarus dead.

And oh ! when I have safely passed
Through every conflict but the last,
Still, Lord, unchanging, watch beside
My dying bed, for Thou hast died ;
Then point to realms of cloudless day,
And wipe the latest tear away.

Sir R. Grant.

125.

CHRISTIAN ! dost thou see them
   On the holy ground,
How the troops of Midian
   Prowl and prowl around ?
Christian ! up and smite them,
   Counting gain but loss :
Smite them by the merit
   Of the Holy Cross !

Christian ! dost thou feel them,
   How they work within,
Striving, tempting, luring,
   Goading into sin ?
Christian ! never tremble,
   Never be down-cast !
Smite them by the virtue
   Of the Lenten Fast !

Christian ! dost thou hear them,
   How they speak thee fair ?
" Always fast and vigil ?
   Always watch and prayer ? "
Christian ! answer boldly,
   " While I breathe I pray : "
Peace shall follow battle,
   Night shall end in day.

" Well I know thy trouble,
   O My servant true ;
Thou art very weary,
   I was weary too :
But that toil shall make thee
   Some day all Mine own,
And the end of sorrow
   Shall be near My throne."

J. M. Neale.
(Translation from the Greek).

126.

ART thou weary, art thou languid,
   Art thou sore distrest?
" Come to me," saith One, "and coming
       Be at rest."

Hath He marks to lead me to Him,
   If He be my Guide?
" In His feet and hands are wound-prints,
       And His side."

Is there diadem, as monarch,
   That His brow adorns?
" Yea, a crown, in very surety,
       But of thorns."

If I find Him, if I follow,
   What His guerdon here?
" Many a sorrow, many a labour,
       Many a tear."

If I still hold closely to Him,
   What hath He at last?
" Sorrow vanquished, labour ended,
       Jordan past."

If I ask Him to receive me,
   Will He say me nay?
" Not till earth, and not till heaven
       Pass away."

Finding, following, keeping, struggling,
   Is He sure to bless?
" Angels, martyrs, prophets, virgins,
       Answer, Yes."

        J. M. Neale.

127.

RIDE on! ride on in majesty!
  Hark! all the tribes Hosanna cry;
O Saviour meek, pursue Thy road,
With palms and scattered garments strowed.

Ride on! ride on in majesty!
In lowly pomp ride on to die!
O Christ, Thy triumphs now begin
O'er captive death and conquered sin.

Ride on! ride on in majesty!
The wingèd squadrons of the sky
Look down with sad and wondering eyes
To see the approaching sacrifice.

Ride on! ride on in majesty!
Thy last and fiercest strife is nigh;
The Father on His sapphire throne
Expects His own Anointed Son.

Ride on! ride on in majesty!
In lowly pomp ride on to die!
Bow Thy meek head to mortal pain,
Then take, O God, Thy power and reign.

Dean Milman.

128.

ALL glory, laud, and honour
   To Thee, Redeemer, King,
To Whom the lips of children
   Made sweet Hosannas ring.
Thou art the King of Israel,
   Thou David's royal Son,
Who in the Lord's Name comest,
   The King and Blessèd One.
              All glory, &c.

The company of angels
   Are praising Thee on high,
And mortal men and all things
   Created make reply.
The people of the Hebrews
   With palms before Thee went ;
Our praise and prayer and anthems
   Before Thee we present.
              All glory, &c.

To Thee before Thy Passion
   They sang their hymns of praise ;
To Thee now high exalted
   Our melody we raise.
Thou didst accept their praises,
   Accept the prayers we bring,
Who in all good delightest,
   Thou good and gracious King.
              All glory, &c.

           J. M. Neale.
        (*Translation from the Latin*
      of Saint Theodulf of Orleans).

129.

WHY doth the Saviour weep
　　At sight of Sion's bowers?
Shows it not fair from yonder steep,
　　Her gorgeous crown of towers?
　　Mark well His holy pains:
　　'Tis not in pride or scorn
That Israel's King with sorrow stains
　　His own triumphal morn.

　　" If thou hadst known, even thou,
　　" At least in this thy day,
" The message of thy peace !　But now
　　" 'Tis past for aye away :
　　" Now foes shall trench thee round,
　　" And lay thee even with earth,
" And dash Thy children to the ground,
　　" Thy glory and thy mirth."

　　And doth the Saviour weep
　　Over His people's sin,
Because we will not let Him keep
　　The souls He died to win?
　　Ye hearts that love the Lord,
　　If at this sight ye burn,
See that in thought, in deed, in word,
　　Ye hate what made Him mourn.

J. Keble.

130.

STABAT Mater dolorosa,
 Juxta crucem lacrimosa,
  Dum pendebat Filius.
Cuius animam gementem,
Contristatam, et dolentem,
  Pertransivit gladius.

O quam tristis et afflicta
Fuit illa benedicta
  Mater Unigeniti !
Quae maerebat, et dolebat,
Pia Mater dum videbat
  Nati poenas inclyti.

Quis est homo, qui non fleret,
Matrem Christi si videret
  In tanto supplicio ?
Quis non posset contristari,
Christi Matrem contemplari
  Dolentem cum Filio ?

Pro peccatis suae gentis
Vidit Jesum in tormentis,
  Et flagellis subditum ;
Vidit suum dulcem natum
Moriendo, desolatum,
  Dum emisit spiritum.

Eia ! Mater, fons amoris,
Me sentire vim doloris
  Fac, ut tecum lugeam.
Fac ut ardeat cor meum
In amando Christum Deum,
  Ut sibi complaceam.

    Ascribed to Pope Innocent III.

131.

AT the Cross her station keeping
　　Stood the mournful Mother weeping,
　Where He hung, the dying Lord ;
For her soul of joy bereavèd,
Bowed with anguish, deeply grievèd,
　Felt the sharp and piercing sword.

Oh ! how sad and sore distressèd
Now was she, that Mother blessèd
　Of the sole-begotten One ;
Deep the woe of her affliction,
When she saw the Crucifixion
　Of her ever-glorious Son.

Who, on Christ's dear Mother gazing
Pierced by anguish so amazing,
　Born of woman, would not weep ?
Who, on Christ's dear Mother thinking
Such a cup of sorrow drinking,
　Would not share her sorrows deep ?

For His people's sins chastisèd,
She beheld her Son despisèd,
　Scourged, and crowned with thorns entwined ;
Saw Him then from judgment taken,
And in death by all forsaken,
　Till His Spirit He resigned.

Jesu, may her deep devotion
Stir in me the same emotion,
　Fount of love, Redeemer kind,
That my heart fresh ardour gaining,
And a purer love attaining,
　May with Thee acceptance find.

Bishop Mant and E. Caswall.

132.

GO to dark Gethsemane,
  Ye that feel the Tempter's power;
Your Redeemer's conflict see,
  Watch with Him one bitter hour:
Turn not from His griefs away;
Learn of Him to watch and pray.

See Him at the judgment-hall,
  Beaten, bound, reviled, arraigned:
See Him meekly bearing all;
  Love to man His soul sustained:
Shun not suffering, shame, or loss;
Learn of Christ to bear the cross.

Calvary's mournful mountain view;
  There the Lord of Glory see
Made a sacrifice for you,
  Dying on the accursèd tree:
" It is finished," hear Him cry;
Learn of Jesus Christ to die.

J. Montgomery.

133.

BOUND upon the accursèd tree,
   Faint and bleeding, Who is He?
By the eyes so pale and dim,
Streaming blood and writhing limb,
By the flesh with scourges torn,
By the crown of twisted thorn,
By the side so deeply pierced,
By the baffled burning thirst,
By the drooping death-dewed brow,
Son of Man! 'tis Thou, 'tis Thou!

Bound upon the accursèd tree,
Sad and dying, Who is He?
By the last and bitter cry
Of expiring agony,
By the lifeless body laid
In the chamber of the dead,
By the mourners come to weep
Where the bones of Jesus sleep,
Crucified! we know Thee now;
Son of Man! 'tis Thou, 'tis Thou!

Bound upon the accursèd tree,
Dread and awful, Who is He?
By the prayer for them that slew,
"Lord, they know not what they do;"
By the spoiled and empty grave,
By the souls He died to save,
By the conquest He hath won,
By the saints before His throne,
By the rainbow round His brow,
Son of God! 'tis Thou, 'tis Thou!

Dean Milman.

134.

THE night of agony hath passed ;
    The day of doom hath dawned at last :
With fainting steps His Cross He bears ;
Foul taunts and curses meet His ears :
The Lord of Life is crucified ;
A felon hangs on either side :
    The people stand beholding.

The powers of darkness do their worst,
The nail, the thorn, the torturing thirst :
Black tempests o'er His spirit break,
" My God, My God, dost Thou forsake ? "
" 'Tis finished ! "   Lo ! He bows His head ;
The Saviour of mankind is dead :
    The people stand beholding.

H. M. Butler.

135.

O SACRED Head, surrounded
  By crown of piercing thorn !
O bleeding Head, so wounded,
  Reviled, and put to scorn !
Death's pallid hue comes o'er Thee,
  The glow of life decays ;
Yet angel-hosts adore Thee,
  And tremble as they gaze.

I see Thy strength and vigour
  All fading in the strife,
And death with cruel rigour
  Bereaving Thee of life :
O agony and dying !
  O love to sinners free !
Jesu ! all grace supplying,
  Oh ! turn Thy face on me !

In this Thy bitter Passion,
  Good Shepherd, think of me
With Thy most sweet compassion,
  Unworthy though I be :
Beneath Thy Cross abiding
  For ever would I rest,
In Thy dear love confiding,
  And with Thy presence blest.

Sir H. W. Baker.
(*Translation from the Latin. Ascribed to
Saint Bernard of Clairvaux*).

136.

O SINNER, lift the eye of faith,
  To true repentance turning;
Bethink thee of the curse of sin,
  Its awful guilt discerning:
Upon the Crucified One look,
And thou shalt read, as in a book,
  What well is worth thy learning.

Look on His head, that bleeding head,
  With crown of thorns surrounded;
Look on His sacred hands and feet,
  Which piercing nails have wounded;
See every limb with scourges rent:
On Him, the Just, the Innocent,
  What malice hath abounded!

O sinner, mark! and count the cost
  Of Love's divine oblation;
Hark! to that loud and bitter cry
  Of loneliest desolation,
"My God, my God, dost Thou forsake?"
That cup was drained for thy dear sake,
  To purchase thy salvation.

J. M. Neale.
(Translation from the Latin).

137.

SON of Man, to Thee we cry ;
  By the holy mystery
Of Thy dwelling here on earth,
By Thy pure and holy birth,
Lord, Thy presence let us see,
Thou our Light and Saviour be !

Lamb of God, to Thee we cry ;
By Thy bitter Agony,
By Thy pangs, to us unknown,
By Thy spirit's parting groan,
Lord, Thy presence let us see,
Thou our Light and Saviour be !

Prince of Life, to Thee we cry ;
By Thy glorious majesty,
By Thy triumph o'er the grave,
By Thy power to help and save,
Lord, Thy presence let us see,
Thou our Light and Saviour be !

Lord of Glory, God Most High,
Man exalted to the sky,
With Thy love our bosom fill,
Help us to perform Thy will ;
Then Thy glory we shall see,
Thou wilt bring us home to Thee.

Bishop Mant.

138.

WHEN I survey the wondrous Cross
   On which the Prince of Glory died,
My richest gain I count but loss,
   And pour contempt on all my pride.

Forbid it, Lord, that I should boast
   Save in the Cross of Christ my God !
All the vain things that charm me most,
   I sacrifice them to His blood.

See, from His head, His hands, His feet,
   Sorrow and love flow mingling down ;
Did e'er such love and sorrow meet,
   Or thorns compose so rich a crown ?

Were the whole realm of nature mine,
   That were an offering far too small :
Love so amazing, so divine,
   Demands my soul, my life, my all.

I. Watts.

139.

THERE is a Fountain filled with blood,
   Drawn from Emmanuel's veins ;
And sinners plunged beneath that flood
   Lose all their guilty stains.

The dying thief rejoiced to see
   That fountain in his day ;
And there may I, as vile as he,
   Wash all my sins away.

Dear dying Lamb, Thy precious blood
   Shall never lose its power,
Till all the ransomed Church of God
   Be saved to sin no more.

E'er since, by faith, I saw the stream
   Thy flowing wounds supply,
Redeeming Love has been my theme,
   And shall be till I die.

Then in a nobler, sweeter song
   I'll sing Thy power to save ;
When this poor lisping, stammering tongue
   Lies silent in the grave.

W. Cowper.

140.

WE sing the praise of Him Who died,
 Of Him Who died upon the Cross ;
The sinner's hope let men deride,
 For this we count the world but loss.

Inscribed upon the Cross we see
 In shining letters "God is Love ; "
He bears our sins upon the tree,
 He brings us mercy from above.

The Cross—it takes our guilt away,
 It holds the fainting spirit up,
It cheers with hope the gloomy day,
 And sweetens every bitter cup.

It makes the coward spirit brave,
 And nerves the feeble arm for fight ;
It takes its terrors from the grave,
 And gilds the bed of death with light :

The balm of life, the cure of woe,
 The measure and the pledge of love,
The sinner's refuge here below,
 The angels' theme in heaven above.

To Christ, Who won for sinners grace
 By bitter grief and anguish sore,
Be praise from all the ransomed race
 For ever and for evermore !

T. Kelly.

141.

"TAKE up thy cross," the Saviour said,
　　" If thou would'st My disciple be ;
Deny thyself, the world forsake,
　　And humbly follow after Me."

Take up thy cross ; let not its weight
　　Fill thy weak spirit with alarm :
His strength shall bear thy spirit up,
　　And brace thy heart, and nerve thine arm.

Take up thy cross, nor heed the shame,
　　Nor let thy foolish pride rebel :
The Lord for thee the cross endured,
　　To save thy soul from death and hell.

Take up thy cross in His dear might,
　　And calmly every danger brave ;
'Twill guide thee to a better home,
　　And lead to victory o'er the grave.

Take up thy cross, and follow Christ,
　　Nor think till death to lay it down ;
For only he who bears the cross
　　May hope to wear the glorious crown.

C. W. Everest.

142.

THERE is a green hill far away,
  Without a city wall,
Where the dear Lord was crucified,
  Who died to save us all.

We may not know, we cannot tell
  What pains He had to bear,
But we believe it was for us
  He hung and suffered there.

He died that we might be forgiven,
  He died to make us good,
That we might go at last to heaven,
  Saved by His precious blood.

There was no other good enough
  To pay the price of sin,
He only could unlock the gate
  Of heaven, and let us in.

Oh! dearly, dearly has He loved,
  And we must love Him too,
And trust in His redeeming blood,
  And try His works to do.

C. F. Alexander.

143.

WHO is this so weak and helpless,
  Child of lowly Hebrew maid,
Rudely in a stable sheltered,
  Coldly in a manger laid?
'Tis the Lord of all creation,
  Who this wondrous path hath trod;
He is God from everlasting,
  And to everlasting God.

Who is this—a Man of sorrows,
  Walking sadly life's hard way,
Homeless, weary, sighing, weeping
  Over sin and Satan's sway?
'Tis our God, our glorious Saviour,
  Who above the starry sky
Now for us a place prepareth,
  Where no tear can dim the eye.

Who is this—behold Him shedding
  Drops of blood upon the ground?
Who is this—despised, rejected,
  Mocked, insulted, beaten, bound?
'Tis our God, Who gifts and graces
  On His Church now poureth down;
Who shall smite in righteous judgment
  All His foes beneath His throne.

Who is this that hangeth dying,
  While the rude world scoffs and scorns?
Numbered with the malefactors,
  Torn with nails, and crowned with thorns?
'Tis the God Who ever liveth
  'Mid the shining ones on high,
In the glorious golden city
  Reigning everlastingly.

Bishop Walsham How.

144.

O COME and mourn with me awhile;
　　O come ye to the Saviour's side;
O come, together let us mourn;
Jesus, our Lord, is crucified.

Have we no tears to shed for Him,
While soldiers scoff and Jews deride?
Ah! look how patiently He hangs;
Jesus, our Lord, is crucified.

How fast His hands and feet are nailed;
His throat with parching thirst is dried;
His failing eyes are dimmed with blood;
Jesus, our Lord, is crucified.

Seven times He spake, seven words of love;
And all three hours His silence cried
For mercy on the souls of men;
Jesus, our Lord, is crucified.

A broken heart, a fount of tears
Ask, and they will not be denied;
Lord Jesus, may we love and weep,
Since Thou for us art crucified.

F. W. Faber.

145.

I GAVE My life for thee,
  My precious blood I shed,
That thou might'st ransomed be,
  And quickened from the dead.
I gave My life for thee;
What hast thou given for Me?

I spent long years for thee,
  In weariness and woe,
That an eternity
  Of joy thou mightest know.
I spent long years for thee;
Hast thou spent one for Me?

I suffered much for thee,
  More than thy tongue can tell,
Of bitterest agony,
  To rescue thee from hell.
I suffered much for thee;
What canst thou bear for Me?

And I have brought to thee,
  Down from My home above,
Salvation full and free,
  My pardon and My love.
Great gifts I brought to thee;
What hast thou brought to Me?

Oh! let thy life be given,
  Thy years for Me be spent,
World-fetters all be riven,
  And joy with suffering blent.
I gave Myself for thee;
Give thou thyself to Me.

F. R. Havergal.

146.

BY Jesus' grave on either hand,
　　While night is brooding o'er the land,
The sad and silent mourners stand.

At last the weary life is o'er,
The agony and conflict sore,
Of Him Who all our sufferings bore.

Deep in the rock's sepulchral shade
The Lord, by Whom the worlds were made,
The Saviour of mankind is laid.

O hearts bereaved and sore distrest,
Here is for you a place of rest ;
Here leave your griefs on Jesus' breast.

So when the Dayspring from on high
Shall chase the night and fill the sky,
Then shall the Lord again draw nigh.

J. G. Smith.

147.

JESUS Christ is risen to-day,   Alleluia !
　　Our triumphant holy day ;   Alleluia !
Who did once upon the Cross   Alleluia !
Suffer to redeem our loss.   Alleluia !

Hymns of praise then let us sing   Alleluia !
Unto Christ our heavenly King,   Alleluia !
Who endured the Cross and grave,   Alleluia !
Sinners to redeem and save.   Alleluia !

But the pains which He endured   Alleluia !
Our salvation have procured :   Alleluia !
Now above the sky He's King,   Alleluia !
Where the angels ever sing   Alleluia !

N. Tate and N. Brady.
(Translation from the Latin).

148.

"CHRIST the Lord is risen to-day,"
　　Sons of men and angels say :
Raise your note of triumph high ;
Sing, ye Heavens, and, Earth, reply !

Love's redeeming work is done,
Fought the fight, the battle won ;
Lo ! our Sun's eclipse is o'er ;
Lo ! He sets in blood no more.

Vain the stone, the watch, the seal ;
Christ hath burst the gates of hell :
Death in vain forbids His rise ;
Christ hath opened Paradise.

Lives again our glorious King ;
Where, O Death, is now thy sting ?
Once He died our souls to save ;
Where thy victory, O Grave ?

Soar we now where Christ hath led,
Following our exalted Head :
Made like Him, like Him we rise ;
Ours the cross, the grave, the skies.

C. Wesley.

149.

JESUS lives ! thy terrors now
    Can no longer, Death, appal us ;
Jesus lives ! by this we know
    Thou, O Grave, canst not enthral us.
                Alleluia !

Jesus lives ! henceforth is death
    But the gate of life immortal :
This shall calm our trembling breath
    When we pass its gloomy portal.
                Alleluia !

Jesus lives ! for us He died ;
    Then, alone to Jesus living,
Pure in heart may we abide,
    Glory to our Saviour giving.
                Alleluia !

Jesus lives ! our hearts know well
    Nought from us His love shall sever ;
Life, nor death, nor powers of hell
    Tear us from His keeping ever.
                Alleluia !

Jesus lives ! to Him the throne
    Over all the world is given :
May we go where He is gone,
    Rest and reign with Him in heaven !
                Alleluia !

F. E. Cox.
(*Translation from the German
of C. F. Gellert*).

150.

ALLELUIA!
   Finita jam sunt proelia,
Est parta jam victoria.
Gaudeamus et canamus   Alleluia!

Post fata mortis barbara
Devicit Jesus Tartara.
Applaudamus et psallamus   Alleluia!

Surrexit die tertia
Caelesti clarus gratia.
Insonemus et cantemus   Alleluia!

Sunt clausa Stygis ostia,
Et caeli patent atria.
Gaudeamus et canamus   Alleluia!

O coronate gloria,
Tua nos morte libera,
Ut vivamus et canamus   Alleluia!

151.

ALLELUIA! ALLELUIA! ALLELUIA!

THE strife is o'er, the battle done,
　　The triumph of the Lord is won;
Oh! let the song of praise be sung.
　　　　　　　　　　Alleluia!

The powers of Death have done their worst,
And Jesus hath His foes dispersed;
Let shouts of praise and joy outburst.
　　　　　　　　　　Alleluia!

On that third morn He rose again
In glorious majesty to reign;
O let us swell the joyful strain.
　　　　　　　　　　Alleluia!

He closed the yawning gates of hell;
The bars from heaven's high portals fell;
Let songs of joy His triumphs tell.
　　　　　　　　　　Alleluia!

Lord, by the stripes which wounded Thee,
From Death's dread sting Thy servants free,
That we may live, and sing to Thee!
　　　　　　　　　　Alleluia!

F. Pott.
(Translation from the Latin).

152.

NOW dawning glows the day of days ;
   All heaven resounds with songs of praise !
From earth loud shouts of triumph rise,
And hell beneath with groans replies.

For He, the mighty King of day,
Hath crushed proud Death's unlawful sway,
And, marching through his dark domain,
Broken the weary prisoner's chain.

Fierce soldiers o'er His tomb kept guard ;
A mighty stone the entrance barred ;
But, bursting from His prison, He rose
Triumphant o'er His baffled foes.

Loosed are the pains of hell this hour ;
Death over life hath lost his power ;
"The Lord is risen," the angel said,
"Why seek the living 'mid the dead ?"

Thou gracious King and Lord of day,
Dwell Thou within our hearts, we pray ;
So from Thine own shall grateful praise
Rise to Thy throne through all our days.

F. J. A. Hort.
(Translation from the Latin.
Ascribed to Saint Ambrose).

153.

ALLELUIA! Alleluia!
   Hearts to heaven and voices raise :
Sing to God a hymn of gladness,
   Sing to God a hymn of praise ;
He, Who on the Cross a Victim,
   For the world's salvation bled,
Jesus Christ, the King of Glory,
   Now is risen from the dead.

Christ is risen, Christ the first-fruits
   Of the holy harvest field,
Which will all its full abundance
   At His second coming yield ;
Then the golden ears of harvest
   Will their heads before Him wave,
Ripened by His glorious sunshine,
   From the furrows of the grave.

Christ is risen, we are risen ;
   Shed upon us heavenly grace,
Rain, and dew, and gleams of glory
   From the brightness of Thy face ;
That we, with our hearts in heaven,
   Here on earth may fruitful be,
And by angel-hands be gathered,
   And be ever, Lord, with Thee.

Alleluia ! Alleluia !
   Glory be to God on high ;
Alleluia to the Saviour,
   Who has gained the victory ;
Alleluia to the Spirit,
   Fount of love and sanctity ;
Alleluia ! Alleluia !
   To the Triune Majesty.

Bishop Christopher Wordsworth.

154.

CHRIST is risen ! Christ is risen !
　He hath burst His bonds in twain ;
Christ is risen ! Christ is risen !
　Alleluia ! swell the strain :
　　For our gain He suffered loss
　　　By divine decree ;
　　He hath died upon the Cross,
　　　But our God is He.
Christ is risen ! Christ is risen !
　He hath burst His bonds in twain ;
Christ is risen ! Christ is risen !
　Alleluia ! swell the strain.

See, the chains of death are broken ;
　Earth below and Heaven above
Joy in each amazing token
　Of His rising, Lord of Love :
　　He for evermore shall reign
　　　By the Father's side,
　　Till He comes to earth again,
　　　Comes to claim His Bride.
Christ is risen ! Christ is risen !
　He hath burst His bonds in twain ;
Christ is risen ! Christ is risen !
　Alleluia ! swell the strain.

Glorious angels downward thronging
　Hail the Lord of all the skies :
Heaven, with joy and holy longing
　For the Word Incarnate, cries,
　　"Christ is risen ! Earth, rejoice,
　　　Gleam, ye starry train,
　　All creation, find a voice ;
　　　He o'er all shall reign."
Christ is risen ! Christ is risen !
　He hath burst His bonds in twain ;
Christ is risen ! Christ is risen !
　O'er the universe to reign.

A. T. Gurney.

155.

THE Head that once was crowned with thorns
  Is crowned with glory now ;
A royal diadem adorns
  The mighty Victor's brow.

The highest place that heaven affords
  Is His, is His by right,
The King of kings, and Lord of lords,
  And heaven's eternal Light ;

The Joy of all who dwell above,
  The Joy of all below,
To whom He manifests His love,
  And grants His Name to know.

To them the Cross, with all its shame,
  With all its grace, is given :
Their name an everlasting name,
  Their joy the joy of heaven.

They suffer with their Lord below,
  They reign with Him above ;
Their profit and their joy to know
  The mystery of His love.

T. Kelly.

156.

AT the Lamb's high feast we sing
  Praise to our victorious King,
Who hath washed us in the tide
Flowing from His piercèd side ;
Praise we Him, Whose love divine
Gives His sacred blood for wine,
Gives His body for the feast,
Christ the Victim, Christ the Priest.

Where the Paschal blood is poured,
Death's dark angel sheathes his sword ;
Israel's hosts triumphant go
Through the wave that drowns the foe.
Praise we Christ, Whose blood was shed,
Paschal Victim, Paschal Bread ;
With sincerity and love
Eat we Manna from above.

Mighty Victim from the sky,
Hell's fierce powers beneath Thee lie ;
Thou hast conquered in the fight,
Thou hast brought us life and light ;
Now no more can death appal,
Now no more the grave enthral ;
Thou hast opened Paradise,
And in Thee Thy saints shall rise.

Easter triumph, Easter joy,
Sin alone can this destroy ;
From sin's power do Thou set free
Souls new-born, O Lord, in Thee.
Hymns of glory and of praise,
Risen Lord, to Thee we raise ;
Holy Father, praise to Thee,
With the Spirit, ever be.

R. Campbell.
(*Translation from the Latin*).

157.

CHRIST is risen ! the Lord is come,
   Bursting from the sealèd tomb ;
Death and hell, in mute dismay,
Render up their mightier Prey.

Christ is risen ! but not alone !
Death, thy kingdom is o'erthrown ;
We shall rise, as He hath risen,
From the deep sepulchral prison.

Heirs of death, and sons of clay,
Long in death's dark thrall we lay
And went down in trembling gloom
To the unawakening tomb.

Heirs of life, and sons of God,
On the path our Captain trod,
Now we hope to soar on high
To the everlasting sky.

Lofty hopes are theirs indeed
Who the Christian's life shall lead ;
Christ's below in faith and love,
Christ's in endless bliss above.

Dean Milman.

158.

THE happy morn is come ;
　　Triumphant o'er the grave
The Saviour leaves the tomb,
　　Omnipotent to save :
Captivity is captive led ;
For Jesus liveth, Who was dead.

Who now accuses them
　　For whom their Surety died ?
Who now shall those condemn
　　Whom God hath justified ?
Captivity is captive led ;
For Jesus liveth, Who was dead.

Christ hath the ransom paid,
　　The glorious work is done ;
On Him our help is laid,
　　By Him our victory won :
Captivity is captive led ;
For Jesus liveth, Who was dead.

Hail ! the triumphant Lord,
　　The Resurrection Thou !
Hail ! the Incarnate Word !
　　Before Thy throne we bow :
Captivity is captive led ;
For Jesus liveth, Who was dead.

T. Haweis.

159.

LIFT up, lift up your voices now,
   The whole wide world rejoices now ;
The Lord hath triumphed gloriously,
The Lord shall reign victoriously.

In vain with stone the cave they barred,
In vain the watch kept ward and guard :
Majestic from the spoilèd tomb
In pomp of triumph Christ is come.

He binds in chains the ancient foe,
A countless host He frees from woe ;
And heaven's high portal open flies,
For Christ has risen, and man shall rise.

And all He did, and all He bare,
He gives us as our own to share ;
And hope and joy and peace begin,
For Christ has won, and man shall win.

O Victor, aid us in the fight,
And lead through death to realms of light ;
We safely pass where Thou hast trod,
In Thee we die, to rise to God.

J. M. Neale.
(Translation from the Latin).

160.

THE Lord of Might from Sinai's brow
   Gave forth His voice of thunder ;
And Israel lay on earth below,
   Outstretched in fear and wonder :
Beneath His feet was pitchy night,
And at His left hand and His right
   The rocks were rent asunder.

The Lord of Love on Calvary,
   A meek and suffering Stranger,
Upraised to heaven His languid eye
   In nature's hour of danger :
For us He bore the weight of woe,
For us He gave His blood to flow,
   And met His Father's anger.

The Lord of Love, the Lord of Might,
   The King of all created,
Shall back return to claim His right,
   On clouds of glory seated ;
With trumpet-sound and angel-song,
And Alleluias loud and long
   O'er death and hell defeated.

Bishop Heber.

161.

WHEN two friends on Easter-Day
    To Emmaus bent their way,
On that Paschal eventide
Christ was walking at their side.
Then their hearts within them glowed
When Himself to them He showed
In the Scriptures as a King
Glorified by suffering.

So Thy presence, Lord, we feel
When we at Thy table kneel ;
When we feed upon Thee there,
We too at Emmaus are,
Then our eyes are openèd
In the break ng of the bread ;
Faith Thee ever present sees
In Thy holy mysteries.

Though not kenned by carnal eye,
Yet we know Thee ever nigh ;
Though Thou art much further gone,
Even to Thy heavenly throne,
Yet we, Lord, behold Thy face
Ever in Thy means of grace ;
There Thou walkest by our side,
There Thou with us dost abide.

        Bishop Christopher Wordsworth.

162.

O GOD, by Whom the seed is given,
By Whom the harvest blest;
Whose Word, like Manna showered from heaven,
Is planted in our breast;

Preserve it from the passing feet,
And plunderers of the air,
The sultry sun's intenser heat,
And weeds of worldly care.

Though buried deep, or thinly strown,
Do Thou Thy grace supply:
The hope in earthly furrows sown
Shall ripen in the sky.

Bishop Heber.

163.

HAIL the day that sees Him rise,	Alleluia !
Glorious, from our wondering eyes !	Alleluia !
Christ, awhile to mortals given,	Alleluia !
Enters now the highest heaven.	Alleluia !
There the glorious triumph waits ;	Alleluia !
Lift your heads, eternal gates :	Alleluia !
Victor over death and sin,	Alleluia !
Comes the King of Glory in.	Alleluia !
Lo ! the heaven its Lord receives ;	Alleluia !
Yet He loves the earth He leaves :	Alleluia !
Though returning to His throne,	Alleluia !
Still He calls mankind His own.	Alleluia !

C. Wesley

164.

THOU art gone up on high
　　To mansions in the skies ;
And round Thy throne unceasingly
　　The songs of praise arise.
　　But we are lingering here,
　　With sin and care oppressed ;
Lord, send Thy promised Comforter,
　　And lead us to our rest.

　　Thou art gone up on high ;
　　But Thou didst first come down,
Through earth's most bitter misery,
　　To travel to Thy crown :
　　And girt with griefs and fears
　　Our onward course must be ;
But only let that path of tears
　　Lead us at last to Thee.

　　Thou art gone up on high ;
　　But Thou shalt come again,
With all the armies of the sky
　　Attendant in Thy train.
　　Oh ! by Thy saving power
　　So make us live and die,
That we may stand in that dread hour
　　At Thy right hand on high.

E. Toke.

165.

THE eternal gates lift up their heads,
   The doors are opened wide ;
The King of Glory is gone up
   Unto His Father's side.

Thou art gone in before us, Lord,
   Thou hast prepared a place,
That we may be where now Thou art,
   And look upon Thy face.

And ever on our earthly path
   A gleam of glory lies ;
A light still breaks behind the cloud
   That veils Thee from our eyes.

Lift up our hearts, lift up our minds,
   And let Thy grace be given,
That, while we linger yet below,
   Our treasure be in heaven :

That, where Thou art at God's right hand,
   Our hope, our love, may be ;
Dwell in us now, that we may dwell
   For evermore in Thee.

C. F. Alexander.

166.

WHERE high the heavenly temple stands,
The house of God not made with hands,
A great High Priest our nature wears,
Jesus, the Son of Man, appears.

He, Who for men their Surety stood,
And poured on earth His precious blood,
Now high exalted for us pleads,
And with His Father intercedes.

He knows—for He hath borne the same—
The wants and frailty of our frame ;
And, though ascended up on high,
Still bends on earth a pitying eye.

Saviour, with boldness to Thy throne
We come to make our sorrows known ;
For mercy and for grace we plead,
To help us in the hour of need.

M. Bruce.

167.

CROWN Him with crowns of gold,
 All nations great and small;
Crown Him, ye martyred saints of old,
 The Lamb once slain for all:
 The Lamb once slain for them
 Who bring their praises now,
As jewels in the diadem
 That girds His sacred brow.

Crown Him the Son of God
 Before the worlds began ;
And ye, who tread where He hath trod,
 Crown Him the Son of Man:
 Who every grief hath known
 That wrings the human breast,
And takes and bears them for His own,
 That all in Him may rest.

Crown Him the Lord of Light,
 Who, on a darkened world,
In robes of glory infinite,
 His fiery flag unfurled ;
 And bore it raised on high,
 In heaven, on earth, beneath,
To all the sign of victory
 O'er Satan, sin, and death.

Crown Him the Lord of Life,
 Who triumphed o'er the grave,
And rose victorious in the strife
 For those He came to save.
 His glories now we sing,
 Who died and rose on high,
Who died, eternal life to bring,
 And lives, that death may die.

       G. Thring.

168

HE is gone—beyond the skies,
    A cloud receives Him from our eyes ;
Gone beyond the highest height
Of mortal gaze or angels' flight ;
Through the veil of time and space
Passed into the Holiest Place ;
All the toil, the sorrow done,
All the battle fought and won.

He is gone—and we remain
In this world of sin and pain ;
In the void which He has left,
On this earth of Him bereft,
We have still His work to do,
We can still His path pursue,
Seek Him both in friend and foe,
In ourselves His image show.

He is gone—we heard Him say,
" Good that I should go away."
Gone is that dear Form and Face,
But not gone His present grace ;
Though Himself no more we see,
Comfortless we cannot be :
No ! His Spirit still is ours,
Quickening, freshening all our powers.

He is gone—towards their goal
World and Church must onward roll ;
Far behind we leave the past,
Forwards are our glances cast :
Still His words before us range
Through the ages, as they change :
Wheresoe'er the Truth shall lead,
He will give whate'er we need.

He is gone—but we once more
Shall behold Him as before ;
In the heaven of heavens the same
As on earth He went and came.
In the many mansions there
Place for us will He prepare :
In that world, unseen, unknown,
He and we may yet be one.

He is gone—but, not in vain,
Wait, until He comes again ;
He is risen, He is not here,
Far above this earthly sphere :
Evermore in heart and mind,
Where our peace in Him we find,
To our own eternal Friend
Thitherward let us ascend.

Dean Stanley.

169.

WE saw Thee not when Thou didst come
  To this poor world of sin and death,
Nor e'er beheld Thy cottage-home
  In that despisèd Nazareth;
But we believe Thy footsteps trod
Its streets and plains, Thou Son of God.

We did not see Thee lifted high
  Amid that wild and savage crew,
Nor heard Thy meek, imploring cry,
  "Forgive, they know not what they do;"
Yet we believe the deed was done,
Which shook the earth and veiled the sun.

We stood not by the empty tomb
  Where late Thy sacred body lay,
Nor sat within that upper room,
  Nor met Thee in the open way;
But we believe that angels said,
"Why seek the living with the dead?"

We did not mark the chosen few
  When Thou didst through the clouds ascend,
First lift to Heaven their wondering view,
  Then to the earth all prostrate bend;
Yet we believe that mortal eyes
Beheld that journey to the skies.

And now that Thou dost reign on high,
  And thence Thy waiting people bless,
No ray of glory from the sky
  Doth shine upon our wilderness;
But we believe Thy faithful word,
And trust in our redeeming Lord.

J. H. Gurney.

170.

OUR Blest Redeemer, ere He breathed
   His tender, last farewell,
A Guide, a Comforter, bequeathed
   With us to dwell.

He came sweet influence to impart,
   A gracious, willing Guest,
While He can find one humble heart,
   Wherein to rest.

And His that gentle voice we hear,
   Soft as the breath of even,
That checks each thought, that calms each fear,
   And speaks of heaven.

And every virtue we possess,
   And every conquest won,
And every thought of holiness
   Are His alone.

Spirit of purity and grace,
   Our weakness pitying see:
Oh! make our hearts Thy dwelling-place,
   And worthier Thee.

Oh! praise the Father; praise the Son;
   Blest Spirit, praise to Thee!
All praise to God, the Three in One,
   The One in Three!

H. Auber.

171.

COME, Holy Ghost, our souls inspire,
   And lighten with celestial fire :
Thou the anointing Spirit art,
Who dost Thy sevenfold gifts impart ;
Thy blessed unction from above
Is comfort, life, and fire of love.

Enable with perpetual light
The dulness of our blinded sight ;
Anoint and cheer our soilèd face
With the abundance of Thy grace :
Keep far our foes, give peace at home ;
Where Thou art Guide no ill can come.

Teach us to know the Father, Son,
And Thee, of both, to be but One ;
That through the ages all along
This may be our endless song :
Praise to Thy eternal merit,
Father, Son, and Holy Spirit !

           Bishop Cosin.
          (Translation from the Latin).

172.

COME, Holy Spirit, come,
    Let Thy bright beams arise:
Dispel the sorrow from our minds,
    The darkness from our eyes.

Convince us all of sin,
    Then lead to Jesu's blood ;
And to our wandering view reveal
    The secret love of God.

Revive our drooping faith,
    Our fears and doubts remove ;
And kindle in our breast the flame
    Of never-dying love.

'Tis Thine to cleanse the heart,
    To sanctify the soul,
To pour fresh life on every part,
    And new create the whole.

J. Hart.

173.

VENI, sancte Spiritus,
Et emitte caelitus
Lucis Tuae radium.

Veni, Pater pauperum,
Veni, Dator munerum,
Veni, Lumen cordium;

Consolator optime,
Dulcis Hospes animae,
Dulce Refrigerium:

In labore Requies,
In aestu Temperies,
In fletu Solatium.

O Lux beatissima,
Reple cordis intima
Tuorum fidelium.

Sine Tuo numine
Nihil est in homine,
Nihil est innoxium.

Lava quod est sordidum,
Riga quod est aridum,
Sana quod est saucium:

Flecte quod est rigidum,
Fove quod est frigidum,
Rege quod est devium.

Da Tuis fidelibus
In Te confidentibus
Sacrum Septenarium;

Da virtutis meritum,
Da salutis exitum,
Da perenne gaudium.

Ascribed to Pope Innocent III.

174.

COME, Thou Holy Ghost, we pray,
    Send from realms of heavenly day
All Thy bright enlivening ray.

Come, Thou Father of the poor,
Come, with gifts that aye endure,
Come, Thou Light of hearts, all pure :

Comforter, of all the best,
Thou the soul's delightsome Guest,
Glad Refreshment, welcome Rest :

Thou, in toil Repose so sweet,
Thou, the Shade in wearying heat,
Thou in sorrow Comfort meet.

Light, most blessed Light Thou art ;
Freely fill in every part
All Thy faithful people's heart.

Save through Thine all-powerful will ;
Man hath nought, can nought fulfil
Nought but what is full of ill.

Wash Thou each defiling stain
Water Thou what needeth rain,
Heal Thou every wound and pain.

Bend the stubborn to Thy sway,
Warm the cold with quickening ray,
Guide the wandering in Thy way.

Give Thou to Thy faithful race,
Who confiding seek Thy face,
All Thy holy sevenfold grace.

Give them virtue's meed, we pray,
Give Redemption's perfect day,
Give the joys that live for aye.

H. J. Buckoll.

175.

WHEN God of old came down from heaven
  In power and wrath He came;
Before His feet the clouds were riven,
  Half darkness and half flame.

But when He came the second time,
  He came in power and love;
Softer than gale at morning prime
  Hovered His holy Dove.

The fires that rushed on Sinai down
  In sudden torrents dread,
Now gently light, a glorious crown,
  On every sainted head.

And as on Israel's awe-struck ear
  The voice exceeding loud,
The trump, that angels quake to hear,
  Thrilled from the deep dark cloud;

So, when the Spirit of our God
  Came down His flock to find,
A voice from heaven was heard abroad,
  A rushing, mighty wind.

It fills the Church of God, It fills
  The sinful world around;
Only in stubborn hearts and wills
  No place for It is found.

Come, Lord, come, Wisdom, Love, and Power,
  Open our ears to hear;
Let us not miss the accepted hour;
  Save, Lord, by love or fear.

J. Keble.

176.

HOLY Spirit, from on high
Bend on us a pitying eye;
Animate the drooping heart,
Bid the power of sin depart.

Light up every dark recess
Of our heart's ungodliness;
Show us every devious way
Where our steps have gone astray.

Teach us with repentant grief
Humbly to implore relief:
Then the Saviour's blood reveal,
All our deep disease to heal.

May we daily grow in grace,
Still pursue the heavenly race,
Trained by Wisdom, led by Love,
Till we reach our rest above.

W. H. Bathurst.

177.

HOLY, Holy, Holy! Lord God Almighty!
    Early in the morning our song shall rise to Thee;
Holy, Holy, Holy! Merciful and Mighty!
God in Three Persons, Blessèd Trinity!

Holy, Holy, Holy! all the saints adore Thee,
Casting down their golden crowns around the glassy sea;
Cherubim and Seraphim falling down before Thee,
Which wert, and art, and evermore shalt be.

Holy, Holy, Holy! though the darkness hide Thee,
Though the eye of sinful man Thy glory may not see,
Only Thou art Holy, there is none beside Thee,
Perfect in power, in love, and purity.

Holy, Holy, Holy! Lord God Almighty!
All Thy works shall praise Thy Name in earth and sky
    and sea;
Holy, Holy, Holy! Merciful and Mighty!
God in Three Persons, Blessèd Trinity!

Bishop Heber.

178.

BRIGHT the vision that delighted
 Once the sight of Judah's seer;
Sweet the countless tongues united
 To entrance the prophet's ear.

Round the Lord in glory seated
 Cherubim and Seraphim
Filled His temple, and repeated
 Each to each the alternate hymn :

" Lord, Thy glory fills the heaven,
 " Earth is with its fulness stored ;
" Unto Thee be glory given,
 " Holy, Holy, Holy, Lord !"

Heaven is still with glory ringing ;
 Earth takes up the angels' cry,
" Holy, Holy, Holy !" singing,
 " Lord of Hosts, the Lord Most High !"

With His Seraph train before Him,
 With His holy Church below,
Thus conspire we to adore Him,
 Bid we thus our anthems flow :

" Lord, Thy glory fills the heaven,
 " Earth is with its fulness stored ;
" Unto Thee be glory given,
 " Holy, Holy, Holy, Lord !"

Bishop Mant.

179.

FATHER of heaven, Whose love profound
    A ransom for our souls hath found,
Before Thy throne we sinners bend;
To us Thy pardoning love extend.

Almighty Son, Incarnate Word,
Our Prophet, Priest, Redeemer, Lord,
Before Thy throne we sinners bend;
To us Thy saving grace extend.

Eternal Spirit, by Whose breath
The soul is raised from sin and death,
Before Thy throne we sinners bend;
To us Thy quickening power extend.

Jehovah, Father, Spirit, Son,
Mysterious Godhead, Three in One,
Before Thy throne we sinners bend;
Grace, pardon, life to us extend.

E. Cooper.

180.

THREE in One, and One in Three,
 Ruler of the earth and sea,
Hear us, while we lift to Thee
  Holy chant and psalm.

Light of lights, with morning shine ;
Lift on us Thy light divine ;
And let charity benign
  Breathe on us her balm.

Light of lights, when falls the even,
Let it close on sin forgiven ;
Fold us in the peace of heaven,
  Shed a holy calm.

Three in One, and One in Three,
Dimly here we worship Thee ;
With the saints hereafter we
  Hope to bear the palm.

G. Rorison.

181.

WHERE art Thou, Lord? With anxious eye
    We pierce the vaulted night;
World after world we see, but Thou
    Art veiled from mortal sight.

Where art Thou, Lord? The riven rock
    Its fossil store displays;
Age after age we track, but Thou
    Dost shun our lingering gaze.

Where art Thou, Lord? The mind of man
    Each secret law unfolds;
On eagle wing Thy world surveys,
    Yet Thine, not Thee, beholds.

Where art Thou, Lord? We wait Thy word;
    Speak, and Thy presence prove:
Yea, now we feel that Thou art near;
    We know Thee when we love.

W. D. Bushell.

182.

HARK! the song of Jubilee,
   Loud as mighty thunders roar,
Or the fulness of the sea
   When it breaks upon the shore.
Alleluia! for the Lord
   God Omnipotent shall reign;
Alleluia! let the word
   Echo round the earth and main.

Alleluia! hark! the sound
   From the centre to the skies
Wakes above, beneath, around,
   All Creation's harmonies.
See Jehovah's banners furled,
   Sheathed His sword; He speaks, 'tis done;
And the kingdoms of this world
   Are the Kingdom of His Son.

He shall reign from pole to pole,
   With illimitable sway;
He shall reign, when like a scroll
   Yonder heavens have passed away.
Then the end—beneath His rod
   Man's last enemy shall fall:
Alleluia! Christ in God,
   God in Christ, is All in all.

J. Montgomery.

183.

LEAD us, heavenly Father, lead us
　　O'er the world's tempestuous sea ;
Guard us, guide us, keep us, feed us,
　For we have no help but Thee ;
　　　Yet possessing
　　　Every blessing,
　If our God our Father be.

Saviour, breathe forgiveness o'er us ;
　All our weakness Thou dost know :
Thou didst tread this earth before us,
　Thou didst feel its keenest woe ;
　　　Lone and dreary,
　　　Faint and weary,
　Through the desert Thou didst go.

Spirit of our God, descending,
　Fill our hearts with heavenly joy,
Love with every passion blending,
　Pleasure that can never cloy :
　　　Thus provided,
　　　Pardoned, guided,
　Nothing can our peace destroy.

J. Edmeston.

184.

WHERE shall we find our mightiest saint,
   The chosen vessel of the Lord?
The soul to dare and never faint,
   The arm to wield the conqueror's sword?

Where shall we find the shepherd meek,
   With heart aflame at tyrant wrong,
Ever the weakest with the weak,
   And still the strongest with the strong?

We find him where we sought him not,
   Chief in the front of Jesus' foes;
There, where the battle rages hot,
   Loudest of all his trumpet blows.

Love-vanquished prisoner of the Cross!
   The love of Christ doth now constrain:
For Christ he counts his glories loss,
   To live is Christ, to die is gain.

O'er land and sea to all mankind
   He bears the flag his Master bore,
Forgetting still the things behind,
   And reaching forth to things before;

No foe to fear, no toil to grudge,
   Self-pledged, till death shall strike him down,
And He, the Lord, the righteous Judge,
   Grant to His saint the martyr crown.

H. M. Butler.

185.

LORD, to Thy holy temple
  Return, return again ;
Come back, and fill with glory
  The hearts and ways of men :
Not as a lowly Infant,
  Unnoticed and unknown,
But in the royal splendour
  Of Thine eternal throne.

O Thou, Whom we delight in,
  The Messenger of love,
Come to Thy temple quickly
  Back from Thy throne above :
But who may bide Thy coming,
  Who hear Thy footstep's tread,
Who stand when Thou appearest,
  Thou Judge of quick and dead ?

Thy Spirit send before Thee,
  Till every heart, restored
By His new life, adore Thee,
  Their only God and Lord :
And make our offerings pleasant
  As in the days of old,
And as in former happy years
  Of which our fathers told.

Come back, and fill Thy temple,
  Built up of human hearts,
With that abiding presence
  Which never more departs :
Come, where the prostrate nations
  Before Thy feet shall fall ;
Come, with Thy holy angels,
  Come back the Lord of all.

J. S. B. Monsell.

186.

LORD ! pour Thy Spirit from on high,
   And Thine ordainèd servants bless ;
Graces and gifts to each supply,
   And clothe Thy priests with righteousness.

Within Thy temple when they stand
   To teach the Truth as taught by Thee,
Saviour, like stars in Thy right hand
   Let all Thy Church's pastors be.

Wisdom and zeal and love impart,
   Firmness and meekness, from above,
To bear Thy people on their heart,
   And love the souls whom Thou dost love.

To watch and pray, and never faint,
   By day and night their guard to keep,
To warn the sinner, cheer the saint,
   To feed Thy lambs and tend Thy sheep.

So, when their work is finished here,
   They may in hope their charge resign ;
So, when their Master shall appear,
   They may with crowns of glory shine.

J. Montgomery.

187.

SHALL we not love thee, Mother dear,
   Whom Jesus loves so well?
And, to His glory, year by year,
   Thy joy and honour tell?

Bound with the curse of sin and shame
   We helpless sinners lay,
Until in tender love He came
   To bear the curse away.

And thee He chose from whom to take
   True flesh His Flesh to be;
In It to suffer for our sake,
   By It to make us free.

O wondrous depth of grace divine
   That He should bend so low!
And, Mary, oh! what joy 'twas thine
   In His dear love to know!

Jesu, the Virgin's holy Son,
   We praise Thee and adore,
Who art with God the Father One,
   And Spirit evermore.

Sir H. W. Baker.

188.

O THOU, Who didst at Pentecost
    Send down from heaven the Holy Ghost,
That He might with Thy Church abide
For ever, to defend and guide;
Illuminate Thy servants, Lord,
The preachers of Thy holy Word.

O may Thy pastors faithful be,
Not labouring for themselves, but Thee:
Give grace to feed with wholesome food
Whom Thou hast purchased by Thy blood,
Thy sheep and lambs, and thus to prove
How dearly they the Shepherd love.

That which Thy holy Scriptures teach,
That, and that only, may they preach;
May they the true foundation lay,
Build gold thereon, not wood or hay;
And meekly preach, in days of strife,
The sermon of a holy life.

Bishop Christopher Wordsworth.

189.

THOU art the Way ; by Thee alone
   From sin and death we flee ;
And he who would the Father seek
   Must seek Him, Lord, by Thee.

Thou art the Truth ; Thy Word alone
   True wisdom can impart ;
Thou only canst inform the mind,
   And purify the heart.

Thou art the Life ; the opening tomb
   Proclaims Thy conquering arm ;
And those who put their trust in Thee
   Nor death nor hell shall harm.

Thou art the Way, the Truth, the Life ;
   Grant us that way to know,
That truth to keep, that life to win
   Whence joys eternal flow.

Bishop Doane.

190.

O SON of God, our Captain of salvation,
　Thyself by suffering schooled to human grief,
We bless Thee for Thy sons of consolation,
　Who follow in the steps of Thee their Chief;

Those whom Thy Spirit's dread vocation severs
　To lead the vanguard of Thy conquering host;
Whose toilsome years are spent in brave endeavours
　To bear Thy saving Name from coast to coast;

Those whose bright faith makes feeble hearts grow
　　　stronger,
　And sends fresh warriors to the great campaign,
Bids the lone convert feel estranged no longer,
　And wins the sundered to be one again;

And all true helpers, patient, kind, and skilful,
　Who shed Thy light across our darkened earth,
Counsel the doubting, and restrain the wilful,
　Soothe the sick bed, and share the children's mirth.

Thus, Lord, Thy Barnabas in memory keeping,
　Still be Thy Church's watchword, "Comfort ye;"
Till in our Father's house shall end our weeping,
　And all our wants be satisfied in Thee.

J. Ellerton.

191.

L O ! from the desert homes,
  Where he hath hid so long,
The new Elias comes,
  In sternest wisdom strong ;
    The voice that cries
      Of Christ from high,
      And judgment nigh
    From opening skies.

Your God e'en now doth stand
  At heaven's opening door ;
His fan is in His hand,
  And He will purge His floor :
    The wheat He claims,
      And with Him stows ;
      The chaff He throws
    To quenchless flames.

Ye haughty mountains, bow
  Your sky-aspiring heads ;
Ye valleys, hiding low,
  Lift up your gentle meads :
    Make His way plain
      Your king before,
      For evermore
    He comes to reign.

May Thy dread voice around,
  Thou harbinger of Light,
On our dull ears still sound,
  Lest here we sleep in night,
    Till judgment come,
      And on our path
      Shall burst the wrath,
    And deathless doom !

J. Williams.
(*Translation from the Latin*
of C. Coffin).

192.

" ART Thou the Healer that should come,
  Or look we for another still ?"
So spake He from the dungeon gloom ;
  His faith was low, his heart was chill.

The voice that cried in saintliest youth
  " Repent ye" to the startled throng ;
The voice that ever spake the truth,
  And boldly chid the tyrant's wrong ;

The voice that owned, "I am not He ;"
  "Why comest Thou to Jordan's flood?
I need to be baptised of Thee ;"
  "Behold the Atoning Lamb of God!"

Now murmurs, faint, and half o'ercome
  With brooding o'er triumphant ill,
"Art Thou the Healer that should come,
  Or look we for another still?"

The Saviour heard His servant's prayer,
  Then turned Him to His daily task ;
The two disciples wondering there
  Unconscious learn the truth they ask.

Foul spirits fled the shuddering frame ;
  The blind man knew His voice, and saw ;
Up rose the palsied and the lame ;
  The deaf ear heard His Ephphatha ;

The leper from his bonds He freed ;
  The dead He raised to life once more ;
And, mightier yet, the Christ indeed,
  He preached the Gospel to the poor.

Then to the messengers alone
  He spake—and spake no other word—
"Go back, and show My servant John
  What ye this day have seen and heard."

H. M. Butler.

193.

"THOU art the Christ, O Lord,
  The Son of God Most High;"
For ever be adored
  That Name in earth and sky,
In which, though mortal strength may fail,
The saints of God at last prevail!

Oh! surely he was blest
  With blessedness unpriced,
Who, taught of God, confessed
  The Godhead in the Christ;
For of Thy Church, Lord, Thou didst own
Thy saint a true foundation-stone.

Thrice was he put to shame,
  Thrice did the dauntless fall;
But oh! that look that came
  From out the judgment-hall!
It pierced and broke the spell-bound heart,
And foiled the tempter's sifting art.

Thrice fallen! thrice restored!
  The bitter lesson learnt,
That heart for Thee, O Lord,
  With triple ardour burnt:
The cross he took he laid not down
Until he grasped the martyr's crown.

O bright triumphant faith!
  O courage void of fears!
O love most strong in death!
  O penitential tears!
By these, Lord, keep us lest we fall,
And make us go where Thou shalt call.

Bishop Walsham How.

194.

" LOVEST thou Me?" the risen Saviour cried,
 "Lovest thou Me Mine other friends above?"
"I love Thee, Lord;" the humbled saint replied,
 "Thou knowest all, Thou knowest that I love."

Can this be he who thrice his Lord disowned?
 Shall he, thrice pardoned, feed his Master's sheep?
O generous trust! O frailty well atoned
 By years of love and toils that never sleep!

Thou, Who the bruisèd reed didst never break,
 Thou, Who the contrite heart wilt not despise,
Who from the sheepfold dost Thy monarchs take,
 And show'st to babes lore hidden from the wise,

We bless Thee, Lord, that, having marked each fall,
 Each trip, each stumble, when our path was steep,
Thou scorn'st us not, but gently, knowing all,
 The sin, the sorrow, biddest, "Feed My sheep."

Lord of my life, King, Master, Brother, Friend,
 Forgotten oft, and oft, though seen, denied,
Yet patient still, and trustful to the end,
 And watching at Thy wayward servant's side,

Grant, when at length Thou makest all things new,
 And truant fancy may no longer rove,
This heart shall cry, and Thou shalt own it true,
 "Thou knowest all, Thou knowest that I love."

H. M. Butler.

195.

TWO brothers freely cast their lot
 With David's royal Son ;
The cost of conquest counting not,
 They deem the battle won.

Brothers in heart, they hope to gain
 An undivided joy,
That man may one with man remain,
 As boy was one with boy.

Christ heard, and willed that James should fall
 First prey of Satan's rage,
John linger out his fellows all,
 And die in bloodless age.

Now they join hands once more above,
 Before the Conqueror's throne :
Thus God grants prayer, but in His love
 Makes times and ways His own.

To God the Father, God the Son,
 And God the Spirit Blest,
By saints on earth be honour done,
 And by the saints at rest !

Cardinal Newman.

196.

By no new path, untried before,
    Thy servants dost Thou lead;
The self-same promise as of yore
    Supports the self-same need.
The Faith for which Thy saints endured
    The dungeon or the stake,
That very Faith, with hearts assured,
    Upon our lips we take.

Though scattered widely left and right,
    And sent to various posts,
One is the battle that we fight
    Beneath one Lord of Hosts.
We know not, we shall never know,
    Our fellow-labourers here;
But they that strive one strife below
    Shall in one joy appear.

They need, O Lord, Thy special grace
    That fight in this world's view;
But in still conflict, face to face,
    Is Satan vanquished too.
One is the end of them that shed
    Their life-blood for Thy Name,
And them that on the dying bed
    Have glorified the same.

J. M. Neale.

197.

FROM fisher's net, from fig-tree's shade,
　God gathers whom He will;
Touched by His grace, all men are made
　His purpose to fulfil.
But not alone from shady nooks
　Fresh with life's noon-tide dew,
From humble walks, or quiet books,
　Calls He His chosen few:

Out of the busiest haunts of life,
　Its most engrossing cares,
Its nightly travail, daily strife,
　Self-woven golden snares,
He for His vineyard doth provide;
　His gentle voice doth move
The world's keen votaries to His side
　With its persuasive love.

So Matthew left his golden gains
　At the great Master's call;
His soul the love of Christ constrains
　Freely to give up all.
The tide of life was at its flow,
　Rose higher day by day;
But he a higher life would know
　Than that which round him lay.

O Saviour, when prosperity
　Makes this world hard to leave,
And all its pomps and vanity
　Their meshes round us weave;
O grant us grace, that to Thy call
　We may obedient be;
And, cheerfully forsaking all,
　May follow only Thee.

J. S. B. Monsell.

198.

AROUND the throne of God a band
Of bright and glorious angels stand;
Sweet harps within their hands they hold,
And on their heads are crowns of gold.

Some wait around Him, ready still
To sing His praise and do His will;
And some, when He commands them, go
To guard His servants here below.

Lord, give Thine angels every day
Command to guide us on our way;
And bid them every evening keep
Their watch around us while we sleep.

So shall no wicked thing draw near,
To do us harm, or cause us fear;
And we shall dwell, when life is past,
With angels round Thy throne at last.

J. M. Neale.

199.

FATHER, before Thy throne of light
  The guardian angels bend,
And ever in Thy presence bright
  Their psalms adoring blend ;
And, casting down each golden crown
  Beside the crystal sea,
With voice and lyre, in happy choir,
  Hymn glory, Lord, to Thee.

And as the rainbow lustre falls
  Athwart their glowing wings,
While Seraph unto Seraph calls,
  And each Thy goodness sings ;
So may we feel, as low we kneel
  To pray Thee for Thy grace,
That Thou art here for all who fear
  The brightness of Thy face.

Here, where the angels see us come
  To worship day by day,
Teach us to seek our heavenly home,
  And love Thee e'en as they ;
Teach us to raise our notes of praise,
  With them Thy love to own,
That boyhood's time and manhood's prime
  Be Thine and Thine alone.

F. W. Farrar.

200.

O YE immortal throng
  Of angels round the throne,
Join with our feeble song
  To make the Saviour known :
    On earth ye knew
      His wondrous grace ;
      His beauteous face
    In heaven ye view.

Ye saw the heaven-born Child
  In human flesh arrayed,
Benevolent and mild,
  While in the manger laid ;
    And praise to God
      And peace on earth,
      For His dear birth,
    Proclaimed aloud.

Ye in the wilderness
  Beheld the tempter spoiled ;
Well known in every dress,
  In every combat foiled ;
    And joyed to crown
      The Victor's head,
      When Satan fled
    Before His frown.

When all arrayed in light
  The shining Conqueror rode,
Ye hailed His rapturous flight
  Up to the throne of God ;
    And waved around
      Your golden wings,
      And struck your strings
    Of sweetest sound.

P. Doddridge.

201.

THEY come, God's messengers of love,
    They come from realms of peace above,
From homes of never-fading light,
From blissful mansions ever bright.

They come to watch around us here,
To soothe our sorrow, calm our fear;
They come to speed us on our way;
God willeth them with us to stay.

But chiefly at its journey's end
'Tis theirs the spirit to befriend,
And whisper to the willing heart,
"O Christian soul, in peace depart."

Blest Jesus, Thou Whose groans and tears
Have sanctified frail nature's fears,
To earth in bitter sorrow weighed
Thou didst not scorn Thine angels' aid.

To us the zeal of angels give,
With love to serve Thee while we live:
To us an angel guard supply
When on the bed of death we lie.

So, when the toils of earth are past,
We may attain to bliss at last,
And with the choirs of angels sing
Glory to the Eternal King.

R. Campbell.

202.

HARK ! hark my soul ! angelic songs are swelling
  O'er earth's green fields and ocean's wave-beat shore :
How sweet the truth those blessèd strains are telling
  Of that new life when sin shall be more !
     Angels of Jesus, angels of light,
     Singing to welcome the pilgrims of the night !

Onward we go, for still we hear them singing,
  "Come, weary souls, for Jesus bids you come."
And through the dark, its echoes sweetly ringing,
  The music of the Gospel leads us home.
     Angels of Jesus, angels of light,
     Singing to welcome the pilgrims of the night !

Far, far away, like bells at evening pealing,
  The voice of Jesus sounds o'er land and sea ;
And laden souls, by thousands meekly stealing,
  Kind Shepherd, turn their weary steps to Thee.
     Angels of Jesus, angels of light,
     Singing to welcome the pilgrims of the night !

Rest comes at length ; though life be long and dreary,
  The day must dawn, and darksome night be past ;
Faith's journey ends in welcome to the weary,
  And heaven, the heart's true home, will come at last.
     Angels of Jesus, angels of light,
     Singing to welcome the pilgrims of the night !

Angels, sing on, your faithful watches keeping,
  Sing us sweet fragments of the songs above ;
Till morning's joy shall end the night of weeping,
  And life's long shadows break in cloudless love.
     Angels of Jesus, angels of light,
     Singing to welcome the pilgrims of the night !

F. W. Faber.

203.

WHAT thanks and praise to Thee we owe,
　　O Priest and Sacrifice divine,
For Thy dear saint through whom we know
　　So many a gracious word of Thine !

Whom Thou didst choose to tell the tale
　　Of all Thy manhood's toils and tears,
And for a moment lift the veil
　　That hides Thy boyhood's spotless years.

How many a soul with guilt oppressed
　　Has learned to hear the joyful sound
In that sweet tale of sin confessed,
　　The Father's love, the lost and found !

How many a child of sin and shame
　　Has refuge found from guilty fears
Through her, who to the Saviour came
　　With costly ointment and with tears !

O happy saint, whose sacred page,
　　So rich in words of truth and love,
Pours on the Church from age to age
　　This healing unction from above ;

The witness of the Saviour's life,
　　The great Apostle's chosen friend
Through weary years of toil and strife,
　　And still found faithful to the end !

Archbishop Maclagan.

204.

THE Church's one Foundation
　Is Jesus Christ her Lord;
She is His new creation
　By water and the Word:
From heaven He came and sought her
　To be His Holy Bride;
With His own blood He bought her,
　And for her life He died.

Elect from every nation,
　Yet one o'er all the earth,
Her charter of salvation
　One Lord, one Faith, one Birth,
One holy Name she blesses,
　Partakes one holy Food,
And to one hope she presses
　With every grace endued.

'Mid toil, and tribulation,
　And tumult of her war,
She waits the consummation
　Of peace for evermore;
Till with the vision glorious
　Her longing eyes are blest,
And the great Church victorious
　Shall be the Church at rest.

Yet she on earth hath union
　With God the Three in One,
And mystic sweet communion
　With those whose rest is won:
O happy ones and holy!
　Lord, give us grace that we
Like them, the meek and lowly,
　On high may dwell with Thee.

S. J. Stone.

205.

COME, let us join our friends above
　　Who have obtained the prize,
And on the eagle wings of love
　　To joys celestial rise.

Let all below in concert sing
　　With those whose work is done ;
For all the servants of our King,
　　In earth and heaven are one.

One family, we dwell n Him,
　　One Church, above, beneath ;
Though now divided by the stream,
　　The narrow stream of death.

One army of the living God,
　　To His command we bow ;
Part of His host have crossed the flood,
　　And part are crossing now.

Oh! that we now might grasp our Guide!
　　Oh! that the word were given!
Come, Lord of Hosts, the waves divide,
　　And land us all in heaven.

C. Wesley.

206.

WHO are these, like stars appearing,
 These, before God's throne who stand?
Each a golden crown is wearing;
 Who are all this glorious band?
  Alleluia! hark, they sing,
  Praising loud their Heavenly King!

Who are these in dazzling brightness,
 Clothed in God's own righteousness;
These, whose robes of purest whiteness
 Shall their lustre still possess,
  Still untouched by time's rude hand?
  Whence come all this glorious band?

These are they who have contended
 For their Saviour's honour long,
Wrestling on till life was ended,
 Following not the sinful throng:
  These, who well the fight sustained,
  Triumph by the Lamb have gained.

These are they whose hearts were riven,
 Oft with woe and anguish tried,
Who in prayer full oft have striven
 With the God they glorified:
  Now, their painful conflict o'er,
  God has bid them weep no more.

F. E. Cox.
(Translation from the German
of H. T. Schenk).

207.

How bright those glorious spirits shine !
　　Whence all their white array?
How came they to the blissful seats
　　Of everlasting day?

Lo ! these are they from sufferings great
　　Who came to realms of light ;
And in the blood of Christ have washed
　　Those robes which shine so bright.

Now with triumphal palms they stand
　　Before the throne on high,
And serve the God they love amidst
　　The glories of the sky.

Hunger and thirst are felt no more,
　　Nor suns with scorching ray ;
God is their Sun, Whose cheering beams
　　Diffuse eternal day.

The Lamb, Who dwells amidst the throne,
　　Shall o'er them still preside,
Feed them with nourishment divine,
　　And all their footsteps guide.

To pastures green He'll lead His flock,
　　Where living streams appear ;
And God the Lord from every eye
　　Shall wipe off every tear.

I. Watts and W. Cameron.

208.

FOR all Thy saints, O Lord,
  Who strove in Thee to live,
Who followed Thee, obeyed, adored,
  Our grateful hymn receive.

For all Thy saints, O Lord,
  Accept our thankful cry,
Who counted Thee their great reward,
  And strove in Thee to die.

They all, in life and death,
  With Thee, their Lord, in view,
Learned by Thy Holy Spirit's breath
  To suffer and to do.

For this Thy Name we bless,
  And humbly pray that we
May follow them in holiness,
  And live and die in Thee.

Bishop Mant.

209.

THE Son of God goes forth to war,
  A kingly crown to gain :
His blood-red banner streams afar ;
  Who follows in His train?

Who best can drink his cup of woe,
  Triumphant over pain,
Who patient bears his cross below,
  He follows in His train.

The martyr first, whose eagle eye
  Could pierce beyond the grave ;
Who saw his Master in the sky,
  And called on Him to save.

Like Him, with pardon on his tongue
  In midst of mortal pain,
He prayed for them that did the wrong :
  Who follows in his train?

A noble army, men and boys,
  The matron and the maid,
Around the Saviour's throne rejoice,
  In robes of light arrayed.

They climbed the steep ascent of heaven,
  Through peril, toil, and pain ;
O God, to us may grace be given
  To follow in their train !

Bishop Heber.

210.

THERE is a blessèd home
　　Beyond this land of woe,
Where trials never come,
　　Nor tears of sorrow flow;
Where faith is lost in sight,
　　And patient hope is crowned,
And everlasting light
　　Its glory throws around.

There is a land of peace,
　　Good angels know it well;
Glad songs that never cease
　　Within its portals swell:
Around its glorious throne
　　Ten thousand saints adore
Christ, with the Father One,
　　And Spirit evermore.

O joy, all joys beyond
　　To see the Lamb Who died,
To see Him there enthroned,
　　By suffering glorified;
To give to Him the praise
　　Of every triumph won,
And sing through endless days
　　The great things He hath done!

Look up, ye saints of God,
　　Nor fear to tread below
The path your Saviour trod
　　Of daily toil and woe.
Wait but a little while
　　In uncomplaining love;
His own most gracious smile
　　Shall welcome you above.

Sir H. W. Baker.

211.

OH ! what, if we are Christ's,
  Is earthly shame or loss ?
Bright shall our crown of glory be
  When we have borne the cross.

Keen was the trial once,
  Bitter the cup of woe,
When martyred saints, baptized in blood,
  Christ's sufferings shared below.

Bright is their glory now,
  Boundless their joy above,
Where, on the bosom of their God,
  They rest in perfect love.

Lord, may that grace be ours,
  Like them in faith to bear
All that of sorrow, grief or pain,
  May be our portion here.

Enough if Thou at last
  The word of blessing give,
And let us rest beneath Thy feet,
  Where saints and angels live.

Sir H. W. Baker.

212.

TEN thousand times ten thousand,
   In sparkling raiment bright,
The armies of the ransomed saints
   Throng up the steeps of light:
'Tis finished! all is finished,
   Their fight with death and sin;
Fling open wide the golden gates,
   And let the victors in.

What rush of Alleluias
   Fills all the earth and sky!
What ringing of a thousand harps
   Bespeaks the triumph nigh!
O day, for which creation
   And all its tribes were made!
O joy, for all its former woes
   A thousand-fold repaid!

Oh! then what raptured greetings
   On Canaan's happy shore,
What knitting severed friendships up,
   Where partings are no more!
Then eyes with joy shall sparkle
   That brimmed with tears of late;
Orphans no longer fatherless,
   Nor widows desolate.

Bring near Thy great salvation,
   Thou Lamb for sinners slain,
Fill up the roll of Thine elect,
   Then take Thy power and reign:
Appear, Desire of nations,
   Thine exiles long for home;
Show in the heavens Thy promised sign;
   Thou Prince and Saviour, come.

Dean Alford.

213.

FOR all the saints who from their labours rest,
  Who Thee by faith before the world confessed,
Thy name, O Jesu, be for ever blest.
                              Alleluia !

Thou wast their Rock, their Fortress, and their Might;
Thou, Lord, their Captain in the well-fought fight;
Thou in the darkness drear their one true Light.
                              Alleluia !

Oh! may Thy soldiers, faithful, true, and bold,
Fight as the saints who nobly fought of old,
And win, with them, the victor's crown of gold.
                              Alleluia !

O blest communion, fellowship divine !
We feebly struggle, they in glory shine;
Yet all are one in Thee, for all are Thine.
                              Alleluia !

And when the strife is fierce, the warfare long,
Steals on the ear the distant triumph song,
And hearts are brave again, and arms are strong.
                              Alleluia !

The golden evening brightens in the west;
Soon, soon to faithful warriors comes their rest:
Sweet is the calm of Paradise the blest.
                              Alleluia !

But lo! there breaks a yet more glorious day;
The saints triumphant rise in bright array:
The King of Glory passes on His way.
                              Alleluia !

From earth's wide bounds, from ocean's farthest coast,
Through gates of pearl streams in the countless host,
Singing to Father, Son, and Holy Ghost
                              Alleluia !

Bishop Walsham How.

214.

L O! round the throne, at God's right hand,
    The saints in countless myriads stand;
Of every tongue redeemed to God,
Arrayed in garments washed in blood.

Through tribulation great they came,
And bore the cross, and scorned the shame:
From all their labours now they rest,
In God's eternal glory blest.

Hunger and thirst they feel no more,
Nor sin, nor pain, nor death deplore;
The tear is wiped from every eye,
And sorrow yields to endless joy.

They see their Saviour face to face,
And sing the triumphs of His grace;
Him day and night they ceaseless praise,
And thus their loud Hosannas raise:

"Worthy the Lamb, for sinners slain,
Through endless years to live and reign!
Thou hast redeemed us by Thy blood,
And made us kings and priests to God."

Ascribed to Rowland Hill.

215.

HARK! the sound of holy voices, chanting at the
crystal sea,
Alleluia, Alleluia, Alleluia! Lord, to Thee;
Multitudes, which none can number, like the stars in
glory stand,
Clothed in white apparel, holding palms of victory in
their hand.

Patriarch, and holy prophet, who prepared the way of
Christ,
King, apostle, saint, confessor, martyr, and evangelist,
Saintly maiden, godly matron, widows who have watched
to prayer,
Joined in holy concert, singing to the Lord of all, are
there.

They have come from tribulation, and have washed their
robes in blood,
Washed them in the blood of Jesus; tried they were,
and firm they stood;
Mocked, afflicted, scourged, imprisoned, stoned, tormented,
slain with sword,
They have conquered death and Satan by the might of
Christ the Lord.

Marching with Thy Cross their banner, they have
  triumphed, following
Thee, the Captain of Salvation, Thee, their Saviour and
  their King :
Gladly, Lord, with Thee they suffered ; gladly, Lord, with
  Thee they died ;
And by death to life immortal they were born and
  glorified.

Now they reign in heavenly glory, now they walk in
  golden light ;
Now they drink, as from a river, holy bliss and infinite ;
Love and peace they taste for ever, and all truth and
  knowledge see
In the beatific vision of the Blessèd Trinity.

God of God, the One-begotten, Light of Light, Emmanuel,
In whose body joined together all the saints for ever
  dwell,
Pour upon us of Thy fulness, that we may for evermore
God the Father, God the Son, and God the Holy Ghost
  adore.

Bishop Christopher Wordsworth.

216.

THE saints of God! their conflict past,
And life's long battle won at last,
No more they need the shield or sword,
They cast them down before their Lord:
O happy saints, for ever blest,
At Jesus' feet how safe your rest!

The saints of God! their wanderings done,
No more their weary course they run;
No more they faint, no more they fall,
No foes oppress, no fears appal:
O happy saints, for ever blest,
In that dear home how sweet your rest!

The saints of God! life's voyage o'er,
Safe landed on that blissful shore,
No stormy tempests now they dread,
No roaring billows lift their head:
O happy saints, for ever blest,
In that calm haven of your rest!

The saints of God their vigil keep
While yet their mortal bodies sleep,
Till from the dust they too shall rise
And soar triumphant to the skies:
O happy saints, rejoice and sing;
He quickly comes, your Lord and King.

O God of saints, to Thee we cry;
O Saviour, plead for us on high;
O Holy Ghost, our Guide and Friend,
Grant us Thy grace till life shall end;
That with all saints our rest may be
In that bright Paradise with Thee.

Archbishop Maclagan.

217.

IN token that thou shalt not fear
  Christ crucified to own,
We print the Cross upon thee here,
  And stamp thee His alone.

In token that thou shalt not blush
  To glory in His Name,
We blazon here upon thy front
  His glory and His shame.

In token that Thou shalt not flinch
  Christ's quarrel to maintain,
But 'neath His banner manfully
  Firm at thy post remain ;

In token that thou too shalt tread
  The path He travelled by,
Endure the cross, despise the shame,
  And sit thee down on high ;

Thus outwardly and visibly
  We seal thee for His own ;
And may the brow that wears His Cross
  Hereafter share His Crown !

Dean Alford.

218.

SOLDIERS of Christ, arise,
　　And put your armour on,
Strong in the strength which God supplies
　Through His Eternal Son.

　Strong in the Lord of Hosts,
　　And in His mighty power;
Who in the strength of Jesus trusts
　Is more than conqueror.

　Stand then in His great might,
　　With all His strength endued;
And take, to arm you for the fight,
　The panoply of God.

　From strength to strength go on,
　　Wrestle and fight and pray;
Tread all the powers of darkness down,
　And win the well-fought day:

　That, having all things done,
　　And all your conflicts past,
Ye may o'ercome through Christ alone
　And stand complete at last.

C. Wesley.

219.

O GOD of Truth, Whose living Word
　　Upholds whate'er has breath,
Look down on Thy created sons
　　Enslaved by sin and death.
Set up Thy standard, Lord, that we,
　　Who claim a heavenly birth,
May march with Thee to smite the lies
　　That vex Thy groaning earth.

And would we join that blest array,
　　And follow in the might
Of Him, the Faithful and the True,
　　In raiment clean and white?
How can we fight for Truth and God,
　　Enthralled to lies and sin?
He who would wage such war on earth
　　Must first be true within.

O God of Truth, for Whom we long,
　　O Thou that hearest prayer,
Do Thine own battle in our hearts,
　　And slay the falsehood there.
So, tried in Thy refining fire,
　　From every lie set free,
In us Thy perfect Truth shall dwell
　　And we may fight for Thee.

T. Hughes.

220.

BEFORE Thine awful presence, Lord,
　　Thy sinful servants bow,
Trembling to speak the solemn word,
　　To frame the sacred vow.

The sins in hours of weakness wrought,
　　The vain things loved before,
The wanton deed, and word, and thought,
　　Lord, we renounce once more.

Once more we vow the holy Faith
　　To keep unstained and true;
Once more we promise unto death
　　Thy holy Will to do.

Again we gird us to the fight,
　　Again we face the foe,
Resolved, beneath Thy banner bright,
　　Where Thou shalt lead to go.

O Father, pardon all the past,
　　Give back Thy wasted grace;
Strengthen us all, while life shall last,
　　To run the heavenward race.

Still let Thy blessèd Spirit's aid
　　Our strength and comfort be:
Then, though we sometimes be afraid,
　　We still will trust in Thee.

Bishop Walsham How.

221.

THINE for ever! God of Love,
    Hear us from Thy throne above:
Thine for ever may we be
Here and in eternity.

Thine for ever! Lord of Life,
Shield us through our earthly strife;
Thou the Life, the Truth, the Way,
Guide us to the realms of day.

Thine for ever! oh! how blest
They who find in Thee their rest!
Saviour, Guardian, heavenly Friend,
O defend us to the end.

Thine for ever! Saviour, keep
These Thy frail and trembling sheep;
Safe alone beneath Thy care,
Let us all Thy goodness share.

Thine for ever! Thou our Guide,
All our wants by Thee supplied,
All our sins by Thee forgiven,
Lead us, Lord, from earth to heaven.

M. F. Maude.

222.

LORD, shall Thy children come to Thee?
   A boon of love divine we seek:
Brought to Thine arms in infancy,
   Ere heart could feel or tongue could speak,
Thy children pray for grace, that they
May come themselves to Thee to-day.

Lord, shall we come? and come again
   Oft as we see yon table spread,
And, tokens of Thy dying pain,
   The Wine poured out, the broken Bread?
Bless, bless, O Lord, Thy children's prayer,
That they may come and find Thee there.

Lord, shall we come? Not thus alone,
   At holy time, in solemn rite,
But every hour till life be flown,
   Through weal or woe, in gloom or light,
Still let us seek Thy grace, that we
In faith, hope, love, confirmed may be.

Lord, shall we come? come yet again?
   Thy children ask one blessing more;
To come, not now alone, but then
   When life and death and time are o'er;
Then, then to come, O Lord, and be
Confirmed in heaven, confirmed by Thee.

Bishop Hinds.

223.

OFT in danger, oft in woe,
 Onward, Christians, onward go!
Fight the fight, maintain the strife,
Strengthened with the Bread of Life.

Onward, Christians, onward go!
Join the war, and face the foe;
Will ye flee in danger's hour?
Know ye not your Captain's power?

Let your drooping hearts be glad;
March, in heavenly armour clad;
Fight, nor think the battle long;
Soon shall victory wake your song.

Let not sorrow dim your eye;
Soon shall every tear be dry:
Let not fears your course impede;
Great your strength, if great your need.

Onward then to battle move;
More than conquerors ye shall prove:
Though opposed by many a foe,
Christian soldiers, onward go!

H. Kirke White and F. S. Fuller-Maitland.

224.

FIGHT the good fight with all thy might,
　　Christ is thy Strength, and Christ thy Right;
Lay hold on life, and it shall be
Thy joy and crown eternally.

Run the straight race through God's good grace,
Lift up thine eyes, and seek His face;
Life with its way before us lies,
Christ is the Path, and Christ the Prize.

Cast care aside, lean on thy Guide;
His boundless mercy will provide;
Trust, and thy trusting soul shall prove
Christ is its Life, and Christ its Love.

Faint not nor fear, His arms are near,
He changeth not, and thou art dear;
Only believe, and thou shalt see
That Christ is All in all to thee.

J. S. B. Monsell.

225.

TAKE my life, and let it be
  Consecrated, Lord, to Thee :
Take my moments and my days ;
Let them flow in ceaseless praise.

Take my hands, and let them move
At the impulse of Thy love :
Take my feet and let them be
Swift and beautiful for Thee.

Take my voice and let me sing
Always, only, for my King :
Take my lips, and let them be
Filled with messages from Thee.

Take my silver and my gold ;
Not a mite would I withhold :
Take my intellect, and use
Every power as Thou shalt choose.

Take my will, and make it Thine ;
It shall be no longer mine :
Take my heart, it is Thine own ;
It shall be Thy royal throne.

Take my love ; my Lord, I pour
At Thy feet its treasure-store :
Take myself, and I will be
Ever, only, all for Thee.

F. R. Havergal.

226.

HARK! angelic voices,
　　High o'er earth and sea,
Call the heir of glory,
　　Call him to be free.

Loyal-hearted soldier,
　　Reckon not the loss;
Christ the Leader calls thee,
　　Warrior of the Cross.

Speed the brave endeavour,
　　Battle with the wrong;
Satan's hosts surround thee,
　　Christian heart, be strong.

Hark! angelic voices,
　　High o'er earth and sea,
Call each ransomed brother,
　　Lord, to follow Thee.

W. D. Bushell.

227.

CHRISTIAN, seek not yet repose ;
 Cast thy dreams of ease away :
Thou art in the midst of foes ;
   "Watch and pray."

Gird thy heavenly armour on,
 Wear it ever, night and day :
Ambushed lies the evil one ;
   "Watch and pray."

Hear the victors who o'ercame ;
 Still they mark each warrior's way ;
All with one sweet voice exclaim
   "Watch and pray."

First and chiefest, hear thy Lord,
 Him thou lovest to obey ;
Hide within thy heart His word,
   "Watch and pray."

Watch, as if on thee alone
 Hung the issue of the day :
Pray, and all thy weakness own ;
   "Watch and pray."

       C. Elliott.

228.

GO forward, Christian soldier!
  Beneath His banner true:
The Lord Himself, thy Leader,
  Shall all thy foes subdue.
His love foretells thy trials;
  He knows thine hourly need;
He can with bread of heaven
  Thy fainting spirit feed.

Go forward, Christian soldier!
  Fear not the secret foe;
Far more o'er thee are watching
  Than human eyes can know:
Trust only Christ, thy Captain;
  Cease not to watch and pray;
Heed not the treacherous voices
  That lure thy soul astray.

Go forward, Christian soldier!
  Nor dream of peaceful rest,
Till Satan's host is vanquished,
  And heaven is all possessed;
Till Christ Himself shall call thee
  To lay thine armour by,
And wear in endless glory
  The crown of victory.

Go forward, Christian soldier!
  Fear not the gathering night:
The Lord has been thy Shelter;
  The Lord will be thy Light.
When morn His face revealeth,
  Thy dangers all are past:
Oh! pray that faith and virtue
  May keep thee to the last.

L. Tuttiett.

229.

MY God, and is Thy Table spread,
  And doth Thy cup with love o'erflow?
Thither be all Thy children led,
  And let them all its sweetness know.

Hail, sacred Feast, which Jesus makes,
  Rich banquet of His Flesh and Blood!
Thrice happy he who here partakes
  That sacred stream, that heavenly food!

Why are its bounties all in vain
  Before unwilling hearts displayed?
Was not for us the Victim slain?
  Are we forbid the children's bread?

Oh! let Thy Table honoured be,
  And furnished well with joyful guests;
And may each soul salvation see
  That here its sacred pledges tastes.

Revive Thy dying Churches, Lord,
  And bid our drooping graces live;
And more that energy afford
  A Saviour's Blood alone can give.

P. Doddridge.

230.

BREAD of the world, in mercy broken,
  Wine of the soul, in mercy shed,
By Whom the words of life were spoken,
  And in Whose death our sins are dead!

Look on the heart by sorrow broken,
  Look on the tears by sinners shed,
And be Thy Feast to us the token
  That by Thy grace our souls are fed!

Bishop Heber.

231.

LO! the Feast is spread to-day;
　　Jesus summons, come away:
From the vanity of life,
From the sounds of mirth or strife,
To the feast by Jesus given,
Come, and taste the Bread of Heaven..

Why, with proud excuse and vain,
Spurn His mercy once again?
From amidst life's social ties,
From the farm and merchandise,
Come, for all is now prepared;
Freely given be freely shared!

Blessèd are the lips that taste
Our Redeemer's Marriage-Feast;
Blessèd, who on Him shall feed,
Bread of Life, and drink indeed;
Blessèd, for their thirst is o'er;
They shall never hunger more.

Dean Alford.

232.

SAVIOUR, we lift our trembling eyes
    To that bright seat where, placed on high,
The great, the atoning Sacrifice
  For us, for all, is ever nigh.

Be Thou our Guard on peril's brink,
  Be Thou our Guide through weal or woe;
And teach us of Thy cup to drink,
  And make us in Thy path to go.

For what is earthly change or loss?
  Thy promises are still our own:
The feeblest frame may bear Thy Cross,
  The lowliest spirit share Thy throne.

233.

O FIRST in sorrow, First in pain,
  Thou Lamb of God for sinners slain,
Messiah, Jesus, Lord of Life,
Thou mighty Victor in the strife,
Our everlasting Priest, art Thou
Pleading Thy death for sinners now.

Eternal Victim, from Thy side
Thy love did pour a crimson tide ;
And still Thy vesture dyed in blood
Gives token of the cleansing flood :
The Lamb for ever slain art Thou,
Pleading Thy death for sinners now.

O Lord of lords, and King of kings,
Thou Sun with healing in Thy wings,
Pour down upon our darkened sight
The brightness of Thy living light :
So may we know Thee, Victim, Priest,
And find Thee in Thy heavenly Feast.

B. H. Kennedy.

234.

ACCORDING to Thy gracious word,
In meek humility,
This will I do, my dying Lord,
I will remember Thee.

Thy Body, broken for my sake,
My bread from heaven shall be;
Thy testamental cup I take,
And thus remember Thee.

When to the Cross I turn mine eyes,
And rest on Calvary,
O Lamb of God, my sacrifice,
I must remember Thee:

Remember Thee, and all Thy pains,
And all Thy love to me;
Yea, while a breath, a pulse remains,
Will I remember Thee.

And when these failing lips grow dumb,
And mind and memory flee,
When Thou shalt in Thy kingdom come,
Jesus, remember me.

J. Montgomery.

235.

O GOD, unseen yet ever near
   Thy Presence may we feel;
And thus inspired with holy fear
   Before Thine Altar kneel.

Here may Thy faithful people know
   The blessings of Thy love;
The streams that through the desert flow,
   The manna from above.

We come, obedient to Thy word,
   To feast on heavenly food;
Our meat, the Body of the Lord,
   Our drink, His precious Blood.

Thus would we all Thy words obey,
   For we, O God, are Thine,
And go rejoicing on our way,
   Renewed with strength divine.

E. Osler.

236.

AND now, O Father, mindful of the love
   That bought us once for all on Calvary's Tree,
And having with us Him that pleads above,
   We here present, we here spread forth to Thee
That only Offering perfect in Thine eyes,
The one true, pure, immortal Sacrifice.

Look, Father, look on His anointed face,
   And only look on us as found in Him;
Look not on our misusings of Thy grace,
   Our prayer so languid, and our faith so dim:
For lo! between our sins and their reward
We set the Passion of Thy Son our Lord.

And then for those, our dearest and our best,
   By this prevailing Presence we appeal;
O fold them closer to Thy mercy's breast,
   O do Thine utmost for their souls' true weal;
From tainting mischief keep them white and clear,
And crown Thy gifts with strength to persevere.

And so we come; O draw us to Thy feet,
   Most patient Saviour, Who canst love us still;
And by this Food, so awful and so sweet,
   Deliver us from every touch of ill:
In Thine own service make us glad and free,
And grant us never more to part with Thee.

W. Bright.

237.

I AM not worthy, Holy Lord,
　That Thou shouldst come to me;
Speak but the word, one gracious word
　Can set the sinner free.

I am not worthy; cold and bare
　The lodging of my soul;
How canst Thou deign to enter there?
　Lord, speak, and make me whole.

I am not worthy; yet, my God,
　How can I say Thee nay;
Thee, Who didst give Thy Flesh and Blood
　My ransom-price to pay?

O come! in this sweet morning hour
　Feed me with Food Divine;
And fill with all Thy love and power
　This worthless heart of mine.

Sir H. W. Baker.

238.

THEE we adore, O hidden Saviour, Thee,
Who in Thy Sacrament dost deign to be;
Both flesh and spirit at Thy Presence fail,
Yet here Thy Presence we devoutly hail.

O blest Memorial of our dying Lord,
Who living Bread to men doth here afford!
O may our souls for ever feed on Thee,
And Thou, O Christ, for ever precious be.

Fountain of goodness, Jesu, Lord and God,
Cleanse us unclean with Thy most cleansing Blood:
Increase our faith and love, that we may know
The hope and peace which from Thy Presence flow.

O Christ, Whom now beneath a veil we see,
May what we thirst for soon our portion be,
To gaze on Thee unveiled, and see Thy face,
The vision of Thy glory and Thy grace.

Bishop Woodford.
(Translation from the Latin
of Saint Thomas of Aquino).

239.

DRAW nigh and take the Body of the Lord,
  And drink the holy Blood for you outpoured.

Saved by that Body and that holy Blood,
With souls refreshed, we render thanks to God.

Salvation's Giver, Christ, the Only Son,
By His dear Cross and Blood the victory won.

Offered was He for greatest and for least,
Himself the Victim, and Himself the Priest.

Victims were offered by the law of old,
Which in a type this heavenly mystery told.

He, Ransomer from death, and Light from shade,
Now gives His holy grace His saints to aid.

Approach ye then with faithful hearts sincere,
And take the safeguard of salvation here.

He, that His saints in this world rules and shields,
To all believers life eternal yields;

With heavenly bread makes them that hunger whole,
Gives living waters to the thirsting soul.

J. M. Neale.
(Translation from the Latin).

240.

HERE, O my Lord, I see Thee face to face;
  Here faith can touch and handle things unseen;
Here would I grasp with firmer hand Thy grace,
  And all my weariness upon Thee lean.

Here would I feed upon the Bread of God;
  Here drink with Thee the royal Wine of heaven;
Here would I lay aside each earthly load,
  Here taste afresh the calm of sin forgiven.

I have no help but Thine; nor do I need
  Another arm save Thine to lean upon;
It is enough, my Lord, enough indeed;
  My strength is in Thy might, Thy might alone.

Mine is the sin, but Thine the righteousness;
  Mine is the guilt, but Thine the cleansing blood:
Here is my robe, my refuge, and my peace—
  Thy blood, Thy righteousness, O Lord, my God.

Too soon we rise; the symbols disappear;
  The feast, though not the love, is past and gone,
The bread and wine remove, but Thou art here,
  Nearer than ever, still my shield and sun.

Feast after feast thus comes and passes by;
  Yet passing points to the glad Feast above,
Giving sweet foretastes of the festal joy,
  The Lamb's great bridal Feast of bliss and love.

H. Bonar.

241.

"TILL He come"—Oh! let the words
　　Linger on the trembling chords;
Let the little while between
In their golden light be seen;
Let us think how heaven and home
Lie beyond that "Till He come."

When the weary ones we love
Enter on their rest above,
Seems the earth so poor and vast,
All our life-joy overcast?
Hush! be every murmur dumb:
It is only, "Till He come."

Clouds and conflicts round us press;
Would we have one sorrow less?
All the sharpness of the Cross,
All that tells the world is loss,
Death, and darkness, and the tomb
Only whisper, "Till He come."

See the Feast of love is spread;
Drink the Wine, and break the Bread,
Sweet memorials, till the Lord
Call us round His heavenly board;
Some from earth, from glory some,
Severed only "Till He come."

Bishop Bickersteth.

242.

BY Christ redeemed, to God restored,
    We keep the memory adored,
And show the death of our dear Lord,
    Until He come.

His Body slain upon the tree,
His Life-Blood, shed for us, we see;
Thus faith shall read the mystery,
    Until He come.

And thus His dark betrayal night
With His last Advent we unite
By one bright chain of loving rite,
    Until He come:

Until the trump of God be heard,
Until the ancient graves be stirred,
And, with the great commanding word,
    The Lord shall come.

O blessèd hope! With this elate
Let not our hearts be desolate,
But, strong in faith and patience, wait
    Until He come.

G. Rawson.

243.

O THOU Who makest souls to shine
  With light from lighter worlds above,
And droppest glistening dew divine
  On all who seek a Saviour's love;

Do Thou Thy benediction give
  On all who teach, on all who learn,
That so Thy Church may holier live,
  And every lamp more brightly burn.

Give those who teach pure hearts and wise,
  Faith, hope, and love, all warmed by prayer;
Themselves first training for the skies,
  They best will raise their people there.

Give those who learn the willing ear,
  The spirit meek, the guileless mind;
Such gifts will make the lowliest here
  Far better than a kingdom find.

O bless the shepherd, bless the sheep,
  That guide and guided both be one,
One in the faithful watch they keep,
  Until this hurrying life be done.

If thus, good Lord, Thy grace be given,
  In Thee to live, in Thee to die,
Before we upward pass to heaven
  We taste our immortality.

Bishop Armstrong.

244.

SOLDIERS of the Cross, arise,
    Gird you with your armour bright:
Mighty are your enemies,
    Hard the battle ye must fight.

'Mid the homes of want and woe,
    Strangers to the living Word,
Let the Saviour's herald go,
    Let the voice of hope be heard.

Where the shadows deepest lie,
    Carry truth's unsullied ray;
Where are crimes of blackest dye
    There the saving sign display.

To the weary and the worn
    Tell of realms where sorrows cease;
To the outcast and forlorn
    Speak of mercy and of peace.

Guard the helpless, seek the strayed,
    Comfort troubles, banish grief;
With the shield of faith arrayed
    Quench the darts of unbelief.

Be the banner still unfurled,
    Bravely wield the Spirit's sword,
Till the kingdoms of the world
    Are the kingdom of the Lord !

Bishop Walsham How.

245.

LORD, Whose temple once did glisten
　　With a monarch's rich supplies,
To our humbler praises listen,
　Bless our willing sacrifice.
Be our freewill offering, given
　To the Father and the Son,
Sweeter in the sight of heaven
　Than the scents of Lebanon.

Clouds and darkness veiled Thy dwelling
　In Thy chosen house of old,
Though the hymn of praise was swelling
　'Mid the pomp of Ophir's gold :
Here Thy love our hearts shall brighten;
　Hence, ye earth-born clouds, away!
Here Thy Spirit shall enlighten,
　Shining to the perfect day.

When our Israel's sore transgression
　Stops the windows of the sky;
When we sink beneath oppression,
　When we see our thousands die;
Father, when we here adore Thee,
　In Thy house our prayer receive;
When we spread our hands before Thee,
　Here behold us, and forgive.

Dean Vaughan.

246.

THOU inevitable day,
    When a voice to me shall say,
"Thou must rise and come away;

"All thine other journeys past,
Gird thee, and make ready fast,
For thy longest and thy last."

Day, deep-hidden from our sight
In impenetrable night,
Who may guess of thee aright?

Art thou distant? art thou near?
Wilt thou seem more dark or clear?
Day with more of hope or fear?

Little skills it where or how,
If thou comest then or now,
With a smooth or angry brow.

Come thou must, and we must die;
Jesus, Saviour, stand Thou by,
When that last sleep seals mine eye.

Archbishop Trench.

247.

THOU Judge of quick and dead,
　　Before Whose bar severe,
With holy joy, or guilty dread,
　　We all shall soon appear;
　　Do Thou our souls prepare
　　For that tremendous Day;
And fill us now with watchful care,
　　And stir us up to pray:

To pray, and wait the hour,
　　That awful hour unknown,
When, robed in majesty and power,
　　Thou shalt from heaven come down,
　　The immortal Son of Man,
　　To judge the human race,
With all Thy Father's dazzling train,
　　With all Thy glorious grace.

To chasten earthly joys,
　　To quicken holy fears,
For ever let the Archangel's voice
　　Be sounding in our ears;
　　The solemn midnight cry,
　　"Ye dead, the Judge is come!
Arise and meet Him in the sky,
　　And hear your instant doom."

Oh! may we thus be found
　　Obedient to His Word,
Attentive to the trumpet's sound,
　　And looking for our Lord.
　　Oh! may we thus ensure
　　Our lot among the blest,
And watch a moment, to secure
　　An everlasting rest.

C. Wesley.

248.

GOD of the living, in Whose eyes
 Unveiled Thy whole creation lies;
All souls are Thine; we must not say
That those are dead who pass away;
From this our world of flesh set free,
We know them living unto Thee.

Not spilt like water on the ground,
Not wrapped in dreamless sleep profound,
Not wandering in unknown despair,
Beyond Thy voice, Thine arm, Thy care;
Not left to lie like fallen tree,
Not dead, but living unto Thee.

Thy Word is true, Thy Will is just;
To Thee we leave them, Lord, in trust;
And bless Thee for the love which gave
Thy Son to fill a human grave,
That none might fear that world to see,
Where all are living unto Thee.

O Giver unto man of breath,
O Holder of the keys of death,
O Quickener of the life within,
Save us from death, the death of sin;
That body, soul and spirit be
For ever living unto Thee.

J. Ellerton.

249.

CHRIST will gather in His own
　　To the place where He is gone,
Where their heart and treasure lie,
Where our life is hid on high.

Day by day the voice saith, "Come,
Enter thine eternal home;"
Asking not if we can spare
This dear friend it summons there.

Had He asked us, well we know
We should cry, "Oh! spare this blow."
Yes, with streaming tears should pray,
"Lord, we love him, let him stay."

But the Lord doth nought amiss;
And, since He hath ordered this,
We have nought to do but still
Rest in silence on His Will.

Many a heart no longer here
Ah! was all too inly dear:
Yet, O Love, 'tis Thou dost call;
Thou wilt be our All in all.

　　　　　　　　　C. Winkworth.
　　　　　(*Translation from the German*
　　　　　　of N. L. von Zinzendorf).

250.

NOW the labourer's task is o'er,
  Now the battle-day is past,
Now upon the farther shore
  Lands the voyager at last:
Father, in Thy gracious keeping
Leave we now Thy servant sleeping.

There the tears of earth are dried,
  There its hidden things are clear,
There the work of life is tried
  By a juster Judge than here:
Father, in Thy gracious keeping
Leave we now Thy servant sleeping.

There the sinful souls, that turn
  To the Cross their dying eyes,
All the love of Christ shall learn
  At His feet in Paradise:
Father, in Thy gracious keeping
Leave we now Thy servant sleeping.

There no more the powers of hell
  Can prevail to mar their peace;
Christ the Lord shall guide them well,
  He Who died for their release:
Father, in Thy gracious keeping
Leave we now Thy servant sleeping.

"Earth to earth, and dust to dust,"
  Calmly now the words we say,
Leaving him to sleep in trust
  Till the Resurrection Day:
Father, in Thy gracious keeping
Leave we now Thy servant sleeping.

J. Ellerton.

251.

THOU art gone to the grave; but we will not deplore
thee,
Though sorrows and darkness encompass the tomb;
Thy Saviour has passed through its portal before thee,
And the lamp of His love is thy guide through the
gloom.

Thou art gone to the grave; we no longer behold thee,
Nor tread the rough paths of the world by thy side;
But the wide arms of Mercy are spread to enfold thee,
And sinners may die, for the Sinless has died.

Thou art gone to the grave; and, its mansion forsaking,
Perchance thy weak spirit in fear lingered long;
But the mild rays of Paradise beamed on thy waking,
And the sound which thou heard'st was the Seraphim's
song.

Thou art gone to the grave; but we will not deplore thee,
Whose God was thy Ransom, thy Guardian and Guide;
He gave thee, He took thee, and He will restore thee,
And Death has no sting, for the Saviour has died.

Bishop Heber.

252.

BRIEF life is here our portion,
  Brief sorrow, short-lived care ;
The life that knows no ending,
  The tearless life, is there.

O happy retribution,
  Short toil, eternal rest !
For mortals and for sinners
  A mansion with the blest !

And now we fight the battle,
  But then shall wear the crown
Of full and everlasting
  And passionless renown :

The God whom now we trust in
  Shall then be seen and known ;
And they who see and know Him
  Shall have Him for their own.

The morning shall awaken,
  The shadows shall decay,
And each true-hearted servant
  Shall shine as doth the day.

There God, our King and Portion,
  In fulness of His grace
Shall we behold for ever,
  And worship face to face.

J. M. Neale.
(Translation from the Latin
of Bernard of Morlaix).

253.

JESUS died for us, and rose again ;
    Therefore are our hopes no longer dim :
Therefore know we that to die is gain,
    For we sleep in Him.

Therefore father, mother, sister, brother,
    Still are ours, for all are still the Lord's :
Wherefore let us comfort one another
    With these blessèd words.

H. M. Butler.

254.

ETERNAL Father, strong to save,
Whose arm hath bound the restless wave,
Who bidd'st the mighty ocean deep
Its own appointed limits keep;
 O hear us when we cry to Thee
 For those in peril on the sea!

O Christ, Whose voice the waters heard
And hushed their raging at Thy word,
Who walkedst on the foaming deep,
And calm amidst its rage didst sleep;
 O hear us when we cry to Thee
 For those in peril on the sea!

O Holy Spirit, Who didst brood
Upon the waters dark and rude,
And bid their angry tumult cease,
And give, for wild confusion, peace;
 O hear us when we cry to Thee
 For those in peril on the sea!

O Trinity of Love and Power,
Our brethren shield in danger's hour;
From rock and tempest, fire and foe,
Protect them wheresoe'er they go:
 Thus evermore shall rise to Thee
 Glad hymns of praise from land and sea.

W. Whiting.

255.

FIERCE raged the tempest o'er the deep,
  Watch did Thine anxious servants keep;
But Thou wast wrapped in guileless sleep,
      Calm and still.

"Save, Lord! we perish," was their cry,
"O save us in our agony!"
Thy word above the storm rose high,
      "Peace, be still."

The wild winds hushed; the angry deep
Sank, like a little child, to sleep;
The sullen billows ceased to leap,
      At Thy will.

So, when our life is clouded o'er,
And storm-winds drift us from the shore,
Say, lest we sink to rise no more,
      "Peace, be still."

G. Thring.

256.

SOULS in heathen darkness lying,
　　Where no light has broken through,
Souls that Jesus bought by dying,
　　Whom His soul in travail knew,
　　　　Thousand voices
　　Call us o'er the waters blue.

Christians, hearken!　None has taught them
　　Of His love so deep and dear;
Of the precious price that bought them,
　　Of the nail, the thorn, the spear:
　　　　Ye who know Him,
　　Guide them from their darkness drear.

Haste, oh! haste, and spread the tidings
　　Wide to earth's remotest strand;
Let no brother's bitter chidings
　　Rise against us, when we stand
　　　　In the Judgment,
　　From some far, forgotten land.

Lo! the hills for harvest whiten
　　All along each distant shore;
Seaward far the islands brighten;
　　Light of nations, lead us o'er:
　　　　When we seek them,
　　Let Thy Spirit go before.

C. F. Alexander.

257.

FROM Greenland's icy mountains,
  From India's coral strand,
Where Afric's sunny fountains
  Roll down their golden sand;
From many an ancient river,
  From many a palmy plain,
They call us to deliver
  Their land from error's chain.

What though the spicy breezes
  Blow soft o'er Ceylon's isle,
Though every prospect pleases,
  And only man is vile?
In vain with lavish kindness
  The gifts of God are strown;
The heathen, in his blindness,
  Bows down to wood and stone.

Can we, whose souls are lighted
  With wisdom from on high,
Can we to men benighted
  The lamp of life deny?
Salvation! O salvation!
  The joyful sound proclaim,
Till each remotest nation
  Has learned Messiah's Name.

Waft, waft, ye winds, His story,
  And you, ye waters, roll,
Till, like a sea of glory,
  It spreads from pole to pole;
Till o'er our ransomed nature
  The Lamb for sinners slain,
Redeemer, King, Creator,
  In bliss returns to reign.

Bishop Heber.

258.

SPREAD, O spread, Thou mighty Word,
Spread the Kingdom of the Lord,
Wheresoe'er His breath has given
Life to beings born for heaven.

Tell them how the Father's Will
Made the world, and keeps it still;
How He sent His Son to save
All who help and comfort crave.

Tell of our Redeemer's love,
Who for ever doth remove,
By His Holy Sacrifice,
All the guilt that on us lies.

Tell them of the Spirit given
Now, to guide us up to heaven,
Strong and holy, just and true,
Working both to will and do.

Word of Life, most pure and strong,
Lo! for Thee the nations long:
Spread, till from its dreary night
All the world awakes to light.

Up! the ripening fields ye see;
Mighty shall the harvest be;
But the reapers still are few,
Great the work they have to do.

Lord of harvest, let there be
Joy and strength to work for Thee,
Till the nations far and near
See Thy light, and learn Thy fear.

C. Winkworth.
*(Translation from the German
of J. F. Bahnmaier).*

259.

THOU, Whose Almighty Word
  Chaos and darkness heard,
And took their flight,
Hear us, we humbly pray,
And, where the Gospel-Day
Sheds not its glorious ray,
  Let there be Light!

Thou, Who didst come to bring
On Thy redeeming wing
  Healing and sight,
Health to the sick in mind,
Sight to the inly blind,
O now to all mankind
  Let there be Light!

Spirit of Truth and Love,
Life-giving Holy Dove,
  Speed forth Thy flight;
Move on the waters' face,
Bearing the lamp of grace,
And in earth's darkest place
  Let there be Light!

Holy and Blessèd Three,
Glorious Trinity,
  Wisdom, Love, Might,
Boundless as ocean's tide,
Rolling in fullest pride,
Through the earth, far and wide,
  Let there be Light!

J. Marriott.

260.

FATHER of mercies, God of Love,
  Whose gifts all creatures share,
The rolling seasons, as they move,
  Proclaim Thy constant care.

When in the bosom of the earth
  The sower hid the grain,
Thy goodness marked its secret birth,
  And sent the early rain.

The spring's sweet influence, Lord, was Thine,
  The seasons knew Thy call;
Thou mad'st the summer suns to shine,
  The summer dews to fall.

The hand unseen that works above
  Matured the swelling grain;
And now the harvest crowns Thy love,
  And plenty fills the plain.

Oh! ne'er may our forgetful hearts
  O'erlook Thy bounteous care;
But what our Father's hand imparts
  Still own in praise and prayer!

A. Flowerdew.

261.

WE plough the fields, and scatter
  The good seed on the land,
But it is fed and watered
  By God's Almighty hand;
He sends the snow in winter,
  The warmth to swell the grain,
The breezes, and the sunshine,
  And soft, refreshing rain.
    All good gifts around us
      Are sent from heaven above,
    Then thank the Lord, oh! thank the Lord
      For all His love.

He only is the Maker
  Of all things near and far;
He paints the wayside flower,
  He lights the evening star;
The winds and waves obey Him,
  By Him the birds are fed;
Much more to us, His children,
  He gives our daily bread.
    All good gifts around us
      Are sent from heaven above,
    Then thank the Lord, oh! thank the Lord
      For all His love.

We thank Thee then, O Father,
  For all things bright and good,
The seed-time and the harvest,
  Our life, our health, our food;
Accept the gifts we offer
  For all Thy love imparts,
And, what Thou most desirest,
  Our humble, thankful hearts.
    All good gifts around us
      Are sent from heaven above,
    Then thank the Lord, oh! thank the Lord
      For all His love.

J. M. Campbell.
(*Translation from the German
of M. Claudius*).

262.

THE sower went forth sowing,
  The seed in secret slept
Through weeks of faith and patience,
  Till out the green blade crept;
And warmed by golden sunshine,
  And fed by silver rain,
At last the fields were whitened
  To harvest once again.
Oh! praise the heavenly Sower,
  Who gave the fruitful seed,
And watched and watered duly,
  And ripened for our need.

Behold! the heavenly Sower
  Goes forth with better seed,
The Word of sure salvation,
  With feet and hands that bleed;
Here in His Church 'tis scattered,
  Our spirits are the soil;
Then let an ample fruitage
  Repay His pain and toil.
Oh! beauteous is the harvest
  Wherein all goodness thrives,
And this the true thanksgiving,
  The first-fruits of our lives.

Within a hallowed acre
  He sows yet other grain,
When peaceful earth receiveth
  The dead He died to gain;
For though the growth be hidden,
  We know that they shall rise;
Yea even now they ripen
  In sunny Paradise.
O summer land of harvest,
  O fields for ever white
With souls that wear Christ's raiment,
  With crowns of golden light!

One day the heavenly Sower
  Shall reap where He hath sown,
And come again rejoicing,
  And with Him bring His own;
And then the fan of judgment
  Shall winnow from His floor
The chaff into the furnace
  That flameth evermore.
O holy, awful Reaper,
  Have mercy in the day
Thou puttest in Thy sickle,
  And cast us not away.

W. St. H. Bourne.

263.

COME, ye thankful people, come,
   Raise the song of harvest-home:
All is safely gathered in,
Ere the winter-storms begin;
God, our Maker, doth provide
For our wants to be supplied;
Come to God's own temple, come;
Raise the song of harvest-home.

All this world is God's own field,
Fruit unto His praise to yield;
Wheat and tares therein are sown,
Unto joy or sorrow grown;
Ripening with a wondrous power
Till the final harvest-hour:
Grant, O Lord of Life, that we
Holy grain and pure may be.

For we know that Thou wilt come,
And wilt take Thy people home;
From Thy field wilt purge away
All that doth offend, that day;
And Thine angels charge at last
In the fire the tares to cast,
But the fruitful ears to store
In Thy garner evermore.

Come then, Lord of Mercy, come,
Bid us sing Thy harvest-home:
Let Thy saints be gathered in,
Free from sorrow, free from sin;
All upon the golden floor
Praising Thee for evermore:
Come, with all Thine angels come;
Bid us sing Thy harvest-home.

Dean Alford.

264.

O LORD of heaven and earth and sea,
　　To Thee all praise and glory be!
How shall we show our love to Thee,
　　　Who givest all?

The golden sunshine, vernal air,
Sweet flowers and fruit, Thy love declare;
When harvests ripen, Thou art there,
　　　Who givest all.

For peaceful homes, and healthful days,
For all the blessings earth displays,
We owe Thee thankfulness and praise,
　　　Who givest all.

For souls redeemed, for sins forgiven,
For means of grace and hopes of heaven,
Father, what can to Thee be given,
　　　Who givest all?

We lose what on ourselves we spend,
We have as treasure without end
Whatever, Lord, to Thee we lend,
　　　Who givest all.

Whatever, Lord, we lend to Thee
Repaid a thousandfold will be;
How gladly should we give to Thee,
　　　Who givest all!

　　　　Bishop Christopher Wordsworth.

265.

HOLY offerings, rich and rare,
    Offerings of praise and prayer,
  Purer life and purpose high,
  Claspèd hands, uplifted eye,
Lowly acts of adoration
To the God of our salvation,
On His altar laid we leave them;
Christ, present them! God, receive them!

  Promises in sorrow made,
  Left, alas! too long unpaid,
  Fervent wishes, earnest thought,
  Never into action wrought,
Long withheld, we now restore them,
On Thy holy altar pour them,
There in trembling faith to leave them;
Christ, present them! God, receive them!

  Sinful thoughts and wilful ways,
  Love of self and human praise,
  Pride of life and lust of eye,
  Worldly pomp and vanity,
Faults that let and will not leave us,
Though their staying sorely grieve us,
Help, oh! help us to outlive them:
Christ, atone for, God, forgive them!

  Homage of each humble heart
  Ere we from Thy house depart;
  Worship fervent, deep and high,
  Adoration, ecstasy;
All that childlike love can render
Of devotion true and tender,
On Thine altar laid we leave them:
Christ, present them! God, receive them!

J. S. B. Monsell.

266.

THINE arm, O Lord, in days of old
　　Was strong to heal and save;
It triumphed o'er disease and death,
　　O'er darkness and the grave:
To Thee they went, the blind, the dumb,
　　The palsied and the lame,
The leper with his tainted life,
　　The sick with fevered frame.

And lo! Thy touch brought life and health,
　　Gave speech, and strength, and sight;
And youth renewed and frenzy calmed
　　Owned Thee, the Lord of Light.
And now, O Lord, be near to bless,
　　Almighty as of yore,
In crowded street, by restless couch,
　　As by Gennesareth's shore.

Be Thou our great Deliverer still,
　　Thou Lord of life and death,
Restore and quicken, soothe and bless
　　With Thine Almighty breath:
To hands that work, and eyes that see,
　　Give wisdom's heavenly lore,
That whole and sick, and weak and strong,
　　May praise Thee evermore.

Dean Plumptre.

267.

GOD the All-terrible! King, Who ordainest
    Great winds Thy clarions, the lightnings Thy
        sword;
Show forth Thy pity on high where Thou reignest:
    Give to us peace in our time, O Lord.

God the Omnipotent! Mighty Avenger,
    Watching invisible, judging unheard,
Doom us not now in the time of our danger:
    Give to us peace in our time, O Lord.

God the All-merciful! Earth hath forsaken
    Thy ways of blessedness, slighted Thy word:
Bid not Thy wrath in its terrors awaken:
    Give to us peace in our time, O Lord.

So shall Thy children, in thankful devotion,
    Laud Him Who saved them from peril abhorred,
Singing in chorus from ocean to ocean,
    Peace to the nations, and praise to the Lord.

H. F. Chorley.

268.

O LORD of Hosts, Almighty King
   Behold the sacrifice we bring;
To every arm Thy strength impart;
Thy Spirit shed through every heart

Wake in our breasts the living fires,
The holy faith that warmed our sires;
Thy hand hath made our nation free,
To die for her is serving Thee.

Be thou a Pillared Flame to show
The midnight snare, the silent foe;
And, when the battle thunders loud
Still guide us in its moving Cloud.

God of all nations, Sovereign Lord,
In Thy dread name we draw the sword;
We lift the meteor-flag on high
That fills with light our troubled sky.

From treason's rent, from murder's stain,
Guard Thou its folds till peace shall reign;
Till fort and field, till shore and sea,
Join our loud anthem, Praise to Thee!

O. W. Holmes.

269.

HELP us, O Lord; behold, we enter
   Upon another year to-day;
In Thee our hopes and thoughts now centre,
   Renew our courage for the way:
New life, new strength, new happiness
We ask of Thee: oh! hear, and bless.

O God, be with us and direct us;
   O God, our plans and hopes inspire;
O God, from thoughts of sin protect us;
   O God, be all our heart's desire;
O God, be in our thoughts each day,
Nor suffer us to fall away.

And grant us, when the year is over,
   Its latest hour in peace may close;
In all things care for us, and cover
   Our head in time of fear and woes;
So may we, when our years are gone,
Appear with joy before Thy throne.

C. Winkworth.
(Translation from the German
of J. Rist).

270.

FATHER, let me dedicate
 All this year to Thee,
In whatever worldly state
 Thou wilt have me be.
Not from sorrow, pain, or care
 Freedom dare I claim;
This alone shall be my prayer,
 Glorify Thy Name.

Can a child presume to choose
 Where or how to live?
Can a Father's love refuse
 All the best to give?
More Thou givest every day
 Than the best can claim,
Nor withholdest aught that may
 Glorify Thy Name.

If in mercy Thou wilt spare
 Joys that yet are mine;
If on life, serene and fair,
 Brighter rays may shine;
Let my glad heart, while it sings,
 Thee in all proclaim,
And, whate'er the future brings,
 Glorify Thy Name.

If Thou callest to the Cross,
 And its shadow come,
Turning all my gain to loss,
 Shrouding heart and home;
Let me think how Thy dear Son
 To His glory came,
And in deepest woe pray on
 "Glorify Thy Name."

L. Tuttiett.

271.

A FEW more years shall roll,
    A few more seasons come,
And we shall be with those that rest
    Asleep within the tomb:
    Then, O my Lord, prepare
    My soul for that great Day;
Oh! wash me in Thy precious blood,
    And take my sins away!

A few more suns shall set
    O'er these dark hills of time,
And we shall be where suns are not,
    A far serener clime:
    Then, O my Lord, prepare
    My soul for that bright Day;
Oh! wash me in Thy precious blood,
    And take my sins away!

A few more storms shall beat
On this wild rocky shore,
And we shall be where tempests cease,
And surges swell no more:
Then, O my Lord, prepare
My soul for that calm Day;
Oh! wash me in Thy precious blood,
And take my sins away!

A few more struggles here,
A few more partings o'er,
A few more toils, a few more tears,
And we shall weep no more:
Then, O my Lord, prepare
My soul for that blest Day;
Oh! wash me in Thy precious blood,
And take my sins away!

'Tis but a little while
And He shall come again,
Who died that we might live, Who lives
That we with Him may reign:
Then, O my Lord, prepare
My soul for that glad Day;
Oh! wash me in Thy precious blood,
And take my sins away!

H. Bonar.

272.

DAYS and moments quickly flying
 Blend the living with the dead;
Soon will you and I be lying
 Each within our narrow bed.

Soon our souls to God Who gave them
 Will have sped their rapid flight:
Able now by grace to save them,
 Oh! that while we can we might!

Jesu, Infinite Redeemer,
 Maker of this mighty frame,
Teach, oh! teach us to remember
 What we are, and whence we came;

Whence we came, and whither wending;
 Soon we must through darkness go,
To inherit bliss unending,
 Or eternity of woe.

Oh! by Thy power grant, Lord, that we
 At our last hour fall not from Thee;
Saved by Thy grace, Thine may we be
 All through the days of eternity.

E. Caswall.

273.

FOR Thy mercy and Thy grace,
  Faithful through another year
Hear our song of thankfulness,
  Father and Redeemer, hear.

In our weakness and distress,
  Rock of strength, be Thou our stay;
In the pathless wilderness
  Be our true and living way.

Who of us death's awful road
  In the coming year shall tread;
With Thy rod and staff, O God,
  Comfort Thou his dying head.

Keep us faithful, keep us pure,
  Keep us evermore thine own;
Help, oh! help us to endure;
  Fit us for the promised crown.

So within thy palace gate
  We shall praise, on golden strings,
Thee, the only Potentate,
  Lord of lords, and King of kings.

H. Downton.

274.

ANOTHER year, another year
   Hath sped its flight on silent wing,
And all that marked its brief career
   Hath passed from mortal reckoning.

For all Thy grace and patient love,
   Exhaustless still, and still the same,
For all our hopes of joy above,
   We laud and bless Thy Holy Name.

We bless Thee for each happy soul,
   Throughout another fleeting year,
Or by Thy quickening grace made whole,
   Or parted in Thy faith and fear.

Still bear with us, and bless us still;
   And, while in this dark world we stay,
Oh! let us love Thy Holy Will!
   Oh! let us keep Thy narrow way!

So, when the rolling stream of time
   Hath opened to a boundless sea,
Loud will we raise that song sublime,
   All honour, glory, power to Thee!

H. Downton.

275.

O GOD, our Help in ages past,
　Our Hope for years to come,
Our Shelter from the stormy blast,
　And our Eternal Home!

Beneath the shadow of Thy throne
　Thy saints have dwelt secure:
Sufficient is Thine arm alone,
　And our defence is sure.

Before the hills in order stood,
　Or earth received her frame,
From everlasting Thou art God,
　To endless years the same.

A thousand ages, in Thy sight,
　Are like an evening gone;
Short as the watch that ends the night
　Before the rising sun.

Time, like an ever-rolling stream,
　Bears all its sons away;
They fly forgotten, as a dream
　Dies at the opening day.

O God, our Help in ages past,
　Our Hope for years to come,
Be Thou our Guard while life shall last,
　And our Eternal Home!

I. Watts.

276.

FATHER, hear Thy children's praises
 For the boon we owe to-day;
Grateful love our heart upraises,
 This our sacrifice to pay:

Thanks for all Thy mercies given,
 Stores of knowledge here unrolled,
Means of grace, and hopes of heaven,
 Unto us, Thy chosen fold.

Lord, Thy servants' spirits turning,
 Mould them by Thy gracious sway
Godliness and all good learning
 May we follow day by day.

May we, these Thy bounties sharing,
 Every talent use aright,
Still by earthly lore preparing,
 Till our faith be turned to sight:

Till, undimmed by dark reflection,
 Face to face shall Christ be shown;
Knowledge rise to full perfection,
 Knowing e'en as we are known.

H. J. Buckoll.

277.

O MERCIFUL and Holy,
  Who still, by steps unknown,
In simple hearts and lowly
  Dost build Thy loftiest throne;
As Thou of old wast near us,
  To bless our Founder's care,
Bow down Thine ear, and hear us,
  In this Thy House of prayer.

For all the faith and daring
  That haunt our ancient Hill,
And patience, and forbearing,
  Tried good, and vanquished ill;
Sweet praise of our dear Mother,
  And, sweeter far than fame,
The love that binds each brother,
  We glorify Thy Name.

For memory's golden treasure,
  Our boyhood's cloudless brow,
Each pure and blameless pleasure,
  Each brave and holy vow;
And friends still clinging nearer
  As sorrows cross our way,
And some by death made dearer,
  We thank Thee, Lord, to-day.

Whate'er Thy Will shall send us,
  If weal or woe betide,
Do Thou, our God, defend us
  Fast anchored by Thy side:
Here firm, though all be drifting,
  May thousands still adore,
Eye, heart, and voice uplifting
  Till time shall be no more.

H. M. Butler.

278.

NOW thank we all our God,
  With heart and hands and voices,
Who wondrous things hath done,
  In Whom His world rejoices;
Who from our mother's arms
  Hath blessed us on our way
With countless gifts of love,
  And still is ours to-day!

Oh! may this bounteous God
  Through all our life be near us,
With ever joyful hearts
  And blessèd peace to cheer us;
And keep us in His grace,
  And guide us when perplext,
And free us from all ills
  In this world and the next!

All praise and thanks to God,
  The Father, now be given,
The Son, and Him Who reigns
  With them in highest heaven,
The One Eternal God,
  Whom Earth and Heaven adore;
For thus it was, is now,
  And shall be evermore!

C. Winkworth.
(Translation from the German
of M. Rinkart).

279.

REJOICE to-day with one accord,
  Sing out with exultation;
Rejoice, and praise our mighty Lord,
  Our Strength and our Salvation:
Our fathers' God was He,
Our God He still shall be;
Our fathers praised His Name,
Our sons shall praise the same:
Let young and old adore Him.

Our House was built in lowly ways,
  But God looked down upon her:
He gave her wealth and length of days,
  And brought us to great honour,
In life, in death, our Guide;
We own no strength beside;
His hosts are round us still
He guards His holy hill:
Our House shall stand for ever.

Sir H. W. Baker and H. M. Butler.

280.

LORD, behold us with Thy blessing,
  Once again assembled here;
Onward be our footsteps pressing,
  In Thy love and faith and fear:
    Still protect us
  By Thy Presence ever near.

For Thy mercy we adore Thee,
  For this rest upon our way:
Lord, again we bow before Thee;
  Speed our labours day by day,
    Mind and spirit
  With Thy choicest gifts array.

Keep the spell of home affection
  Still alive in every heart;
May its power, with mild direction,
  Draw our love from self apart,
    Till Thy children
  Feel that Thou their Father art.

Break temptation's fatal power,
  Shielding all with guardian care,
Safe in every careless hour,
  Safe from sloth and sensual snare:
    Thou, our Saviour,
  Still our failing strength repair.

H. J. Buckoll.

281.

LORD, dismiss us with Thy blessing,
    Thanks for mercies past receive;
Pardon all, their faults confessing;
    Time that's lost may all retrieve;
      May Thy children
    Ne'er again Thy Spirit grieve.

Bless Thou all our days of leisure;
    Help us selfish lures to flee;
Sanctify our every pleasure,
    Pure and blameless may it be;
      May our gladness
    Draw us evermore to Thee.

May Thy kindly influence cherish
    All the good we here have gained;
May all taint of evil perish,
    By Thy mightier power restrained;
      Seek we ever
    Knowledge pure and love unfeigned.

Let Thy Father-hand be shielding
    All who here shall meet no more;
May their seed-time past be yielding
    Year by year a richer store;
      Those returning
    Make more faithful than before.

H. J. Buckoll.

282.

O GOD of Bethel, by Whose hand
  Thy people still are fed;
Who through this weary pilgrimage
  Hast all our fathers led;

Our vows, our prayers, we now present
  Before Thy throne of grace;
God of our fathers, be the God
  Of their succeeding race.

Through each perplexing path of life
  Our wandering footsteps guide;
Give us each day our daily bread,
  And raiment fit provide.

Oh! spread Thy covering wings around,
  Till all our wanderings cease,
And at our Father's loved abode
  Our souls arrive in peace.

Such blessings from Thy gracious hand
  Our humble prayers implore;
And Thou shalt be our chosen God,
  And portion evermore.

P. Doddridge and J. Logan.

283.

BY cool Siloam's shady rill
  How sweet the lily grows!
How sweet the breath beneath the hill
  Of Sharon's dewy rose!

Lo! such the child whose early feet
  The paths of peace have trod;
Whose secret heart, with influence sweet,
  Is upward drawn to God.

By cool Siloam's shady rill
  The lily must decay;
The rose that blooms beneath the hill
  Must shortly fade away.

And soon, too soon, the wintry hour
  Of man's maturer age
Will shake the soul with sorrow's power,
  And stormy passion's rage.

O Thou, Whose infant feet were found
  Within Thy Father's shrine,
Whose years, with changeless virtue crowned,
  Were all alike divine;

Dependent on Thy bounteous breath,
  We seek Thy grace alone,
In childhood, manhood, age and death,
  To keep us still Thine own.

Bishop Heber.

284.

WHO shall ascend to the Holy Place,
 And stand on the Holy Hill?
Who shall the boundless realms of space
 With shouts of rapture thrill?
  Alleluia!
For the Lord God Omnipotent reigneth!

The servants of the Lord are they,
 The pure in heart and hand,
For whom the eternal bars give way,
 The eternal gates expand!
  Alleluia!
For the Lord God Omnipotent reigneth!

Not to the noble, not to the strong,
 To the wealthy, or the wise,
Is given a part in that angel-song,
 That music of the skies.
  Alleluia!
For the Lord God Omnipotent reigneth!

But those who in humble and holy fear,
 With childlike faith and love,
Have served the Lord as their Master here,
 Shall praise their Lord above.
  Alleluia!
For the Lord God Omnipotent reigneth!

T. E. Hankinson.

285.

FATHER, I know that all my life
   Is portioned out for me;
The changes that are sure to come
   I do not fear to see;
I ask Thee for a quiet mind,
   Intent on pleasing Thee.

I ask Thee for a thoughtful love,
   Through constant watching wise,
To meet the glad with joyful smiles,
   And wipe the weeping eyes;
A heart at leisure from itself
   To soothe and sympathise.

I would not have the restless will
   That hurries to and fro,
Seeking for some great thing to do,
   Or secret thing to know:
I would be treated as a child,
   And guided where I go.

Wherever in the world I am,
   In whatsoe'er estate,
I have a fellowship with hearts
   To keep and cultivate;
A work of lowly love to do
   For Him on Whom I wait.

A. L. Waring.

286.

THY way, not mine, O Lord,
　However dark it be!
Lead me by Thine own hand,
　Choose out the path for me.

Smooth let it be or rough,
　It will be still the best;
Winding or straight, it leads
　Right onward to Thy rest.

I dare not choose my lot;
　I would not, if I might:
Choose Thou for me, my God;
　So shall I walk aright.

Choose Thou for me my friends,
　My sickness or my health;
Choose Thou my cares for me,
　My poverty or wealth.

Not mine, not mine the choice
　In things or great or small:
Be Thou my Guide, my Strength,
　My Wisdom and my All!

H. Bonar.

287.

MY soul, repeat His praise,
　　Whose mercies are so great;
Whose anger is so slow to rise,
　　So ready to abate.

　　High as the heavens are raised
　　Above the ground we tread,
So far the riches of His grace
　　Our highest thoughts exceed.

　　The pity of the Lord
　　To those that fear His Name
Is such as tender parents feel;
　　He knows our feeble frame.

　　He knows we are but dust,
　　Scattered with every breath;
His anger, like a rising wind,
　　Can send us swift to death.

　　Our days are as the grass,
　　Or like the morning flower;
If one sharp blast sweep o'er the field
　　It withers in an hour.

　　But Thy compassions, Lord,
　　To endless years endure;
And children's children ever find
　　The Word of promise sure.

I. Watts.

288.

NEARER, my God, to Thee,
   Nearer to Thee!
E'en though it be a cross
   That raiseth me;
Still all my song shall be,
Nearer, my God, to Thee,
   Nearer to Thee!

Though, like the wanderer,
   The sun gone down,
Darkness comes over me,
   My rest a stone,
Yet in my dreams I'd be
Nearer, my God, to Thee,
   Nearer to Thee!

There let my way appear
   Steps unto heaven,
All that Thou sendest me
   In mercy given;
Angels to beckon me
Nearer, my God, to Thee,
   Nearer to Thee!

Then with my waking thoughts
   Bright with Thy praise,
Out of my stony griefs
   Bethels I'll raise;
So by my woes to be
Nearer, my God, to Thee,
   Nearer to Thee!

And when on joyful wing
 Cleaving the sky,
Sun, moon and stars forgot,
 Upwards I fly,
Still all my song shall be,
Nearer, my God, to Thee,
 Nearer to Thee!

S. F. Adams.

289.

GOD is Love; His mercy brightens
 All the paths in which we move:
Bliss He forms, and woe He lightens;
 God is Light, and God is Love.

Chance and change are busy ever,
 Worlds decay, and ages move:
But His mercy waneth never;
 God is Light, and God is Love.

E'en the hour that darkest seemeth
 Will His changeless goodness prove:
From the mist His brightness streameth;
 God is Light, and God is Love.

He with earthly cares entwineth
 Hope and comfort from above:
Everywhere His glory shineth;
 God is Light, and God is Love.

Sir J. Bowring.

290.

A SAFE Stronghold our God is still,
  A trusty Shield and Weapon;
He'll help us clear from all the ill
  That in our days shall happen.
The ancient Prince of Hell
Hath risen with purpose fell;
Strong mail of craft and power
He weareth in this hour;
On earth is not his fellow.

With force of arms we nothing can,
  Full soon we were down-ridden;
But for us fights the proper Man,
  Whom God Himself hath bidden.
Ask ye, Who is this same?
Christ Jesus is His Name,
The Lord Zebaoth's Son;
He, and no other one,
Shall conquer in the battle.

And were this world all devils o'er
  And watching to devour us,
We lay it not to heart so sore;
  Not they can overpower us.
And let the Prince of Ill
Look grim as e'er he will,
He harms us not a whit:
For why? His doom is writ;
A word shall quickly slay him.

God's Word, for all their craft and force,
  One moment will not linger,
But, spite of hell, shall have its course;
  'Tis written by His finger.
And though they take our life,
Goods, honour, children, wife,
Yet is their profit small;
These things shall vanish all,
The City of God remaineth.

T. Carlyle.
*(Translation from the German
of Martin Luther).*

291.

GOD is our Refuge, tried and proved,
    Amid a stormy world:
We will not fear, though earth be moved,
  And hills in ocean hurled.

The waves may roar, the mountains shake,
  Our comforts shall not cease:
The Lord His saints will not forsake,
  The Lord will give us peace.

A gentle stream of hope and love
  To us shall ever flow;
It issues from His throne above,
  It cheers His Church below.

When earth and hell against us came,
  He spake, and quelled their powers:
The Lord of Hosts is still the same,
  The God of Grace is ours.

H. F. Lyte.

292.

THROUGH all the changing scenes of life,
　　In trouble and in joy,
The praises of my God shall still
　　My heart and tongue employ.

Of His deliverance I will boast,
　　Till all that are distressed
From my example comfort take,
　　And charm their griefs to rest.

Oh! magnify the Lord with me,
　　With me exalt His Name;
When in distress to Him I called,
　　He to my rescue came.

The hosts of God encamp around
　　The dwellings of the just;
Deliverance He affords to all
　　Who on His succour trust.

Oh! make but trial of His love;
　　Experience will decide
How blest are they, and only they,
　　Who in His truth confide.

N. Tate and N. Brady.

293.

WHEN all Thy mercies, O my God,
  My rising soul surveys,
Transported with the view, I'm lost
  In wonder, love, and praise.

Thy Providence my life sustained,
  And all my wants redressed,
When in the silent womb I lay,
  And hung upon the breast.

Unnumbered comforts to my soul
  Thy tender care bestowed,
Before my infant heart conceived
  From Whom those comforts flowed.

Ten thousand thousand precious gifts
  My daily thanks employ ;
Nor is the least a cheerful heart,
  That tastes those gifts with joy.

Through every period of my life
  Thy goodness I'll pursue ;
And after death, in distant worlds,
  The glorious theme renew.

J. Addison.

294.

HOW are Thy servants blest, O Lord!
 How sure is their defence!
Eternal Wisdom is their guide,
 Their help Omnipotence.

In foreign realms and lands remote,
 Supported by Thy care,
Through burning climes they pass unhurt,
 And breathe in tainted air.

When by the dreadful tempest borne
 High on the broken wave,
They know Thou art not slow to hear,
 Nor impotent to save.

The storm is laid, the winds retire,
 Obedient to Thy will;
The sea, that roars at Thy command,
 At Thy command is still.

Our life, while Thou preserv'st that life,
 Thy sacrifice shall be;
And death, when death shall be our lot,
 Shall join our souls to Thee.

J. Addison.

295.

CAST thy burden on the Lord,
    Lean thou only on His word:
Ever He will be thy stay,
Though all else shall melt away.

Ever in the raging storm
Thou shalt see His cheering Form,
Hear His pledge of coming aid:
"It is I, be not afraid."

Cast thy burden at His feet,
Linger near the Mercy-seat:
He will lead thee by the hand
Gently to the better land.

He will gird thee by His power
In thy weary, fainting hour:
Lean, then, loving on His word,
Cast thy burden on the Lord.

J. Cennick.

296.

ALL praise and thanks to God Most High,
  The Father of all Love,
The God Who doeth wondrously,
  The God Who reigns above!

I sought Him in my hour of need,
  "Lord God, now hear my prayer."
For death He gave me life indeed,
  And comfort for despair.

The Lord is never far away,
  Nor sundered from His flock;
He is their Refuge and their Stay,
  Their Peace, their Trust, their Rock.

And when earth cannot comfort more,
  Nor earthly friends avail,
The Father comes Himself with store
  Of help that cannot fail.

O Thou that doest all things well
  In earth and sky and sea,
These lips shall never cease to tell
  What Thou hast done for me.

C. Winkworth.
(Translation from the German
of J. J. Schütz).

297.

GOD moves in a mysterious way
   His wonders to perform;
He plants His footsteps in the sea,
   And rides upon the storm.

Deep in unfathomable mines
   Of never-failing skill
He treasures up His bright designs,
   And works His sovereign Will.

Ye fearful saints, fresh courage take;
   The clouds ye so much dread
Are big with mercy, and shall break
   In blessings on your head.

Judge not the Lord by feeble sense,
   But trust Him for His grace;
Behind a frowning providence
   He hides a smiling face.

Blind unbelief is sure to err
   And scan His work in vain;
God is His own interpreter,
   And He will make it plain.

W. Cowper.

298.

PUT thou thy trust in God,
　In duty's path go on;
Walk in His strength with faith and hope,
　So shall thy work be done.

Commit thy ways to Him,
　Thy works into His hands,
And rest on His unchanging Word,
　Who heaven and earth commands.

Though years on years roll on,
　His covenant shall endure;
Though clouds and darkness hide His path,
　The promised grace is sure.

Through waves, and clouds, and storms,
　His power will clear thy way:
Wait thou His time; the darkest night
　Shall end in brightest day.

J. Wesley.
(Translation from the German
of P. Gerhardt).

299.

" IN the mount it shall be seen;"
 God will all provide:
None have e'er forsaken been
 Who on Him relied.
Fear not; Jesus' aid implore,
Soon will He the light restore.

Out of darkness He will raise
 Soon the dawning day:
Now prepare thy joyful praise,
 He is on His way.
Whilst we seek Him, lo! He brings
Plenteous healing in His wings.

Praise, O Jesu, praise to Thee,
 Who our ills hast borne:
Let Thy word our comfort be,
 " Blest are they that mourn."
Blest are they whom Thou dost bless,
Present Help in all distress.

A. T. Russell.

300.

GOD the Lord a King remaineth,
 Robed in His own glorious light:
God hath robed Him, and He reigneth;
 He hath girded Him with might.
   Alleluia!
 God is King in depth and height.

In her everlasting station
 Earth is poised, to swerve no more:
Thou hast laid Thy throne's foundation
 From all time where thought can soar.
   Alleluia!
 Lord, Thou art for evermore.

With all tones of waters blending
 Glorious is the breaking deep:
Glorious, beauteous without ending,
 God, Who reigns on heaven's high steep.
   Alleluia!
 Songs of ocean never sleep.

Lord, the words Thy lips are telling
 Are the perfect verity:
Of Thine high eternal dwelling
 Holiness shall inmate be.
   Alleluia!
 Pure is all that lives with Thee.

J. Keble.

301.

THE Lord my pasture shall prepare,
   And feed me with a shepherd's care;
His presence shall my wants supply,
And guard me with a watchful eye;
My noonday walks He shall attend,
And all my midnight hours defend.

When in the sultry glebe I faint,
Or on the thirsty mountain pant,
To fertile vales and dewy meads
My weary wandering steps He leads,
Where peaceful rivers, soft and slow,
Amid the verdant landscape flow.

Though in a bare and rugged way
Through devious, lonely wilds I stray,
His bounty shall my pains beguile;
The barren wilderness shall smile,
With sudden green and herbage crowned,
And streams shall murmur all around.

Though in the paths of death I tread,
With gloomy horrors overspread,
My steadfast heart shall fear no ill,
For Thou, O Lord, art with me still:
Thy friendly crook shall give me aid,
And guide me through the dreadful shade.

J. Addison.

302.

THE King of Love my Shepherd is,
　　Whose goodness faileth never;
I nothing lack if I am His
　　And He is mine for ever.

Where streams of living water flow
　　My ransomed soul He leadeth,
And, where the verdant pastures grow,
　　With food celestial feedeth.

Perverse and foolish oft I strayed,
　　But yet in love He sought me,
And on His shoulder gently laid,
　　And home, rejoicing, brought me.

In death's dark vale I fear no ill
　　With Thee, dear Lord, beside me;
Thy rod and staff my comfort still,
　　Thy Cross before to guide me.

Thou spread'st a Table in my sight,
　　Thy Unction grace bestoweth;
And, oh! what transport of delight
　　From Thy pure Chalice floweth!

And so through all the length of days
　　Thy goodness faileth never;
Good Shepherd, may I sing Thy praise
　　Within Thy House for ever.

Sir H. W. Baker.

303.

TRY us, O God, and search the ground
  Of every sinful heart ;
Whate'er of sin in us is found,
  O bid it all depart.

When to the right or left we stray,
  Leave us not comfortless ;
But guide our feet into the way
  Of everlasting peace.

Help us to help each other, Lord,
  Each other's cross to bear ;
Let each his friendly aid afford,
  And feel his brother's care.

Help us to build each other up,
  Help us ourselves to prove ;
Increase our faith, confirm our hope,
  And perfect us in love.

C. Wesley.

304.

LORD, Thy Word abideth,
  And our footsteps guideth;
Who its truth believeth
Light and joy receiveth.

When our foes are near us,
Then Thy Word doth cheer us,
Word of consolation,
Message of salvation.

When the storms are o'er us,
And dark clouds before us,
Then its light directeth,
And our way protecteth.

Who can tell the pleasure,
Who recount the treasure,
By Thy Word imparted
To the simple-hearted?

Word of Mercy, giving
Succour to the living;
Word of Life, supplying
Comfort to the dying!

Oh! that we, discerning
Its most holy learning,
Lord, may love and fear Thee,
Evermore be near Thee!

Sir H. W. Baker.

305.

FATHER of mercies, in Thy Word
  What endless glory shines!
For ever be Thy Name adored
  For these celestial lines!

Here may the wretched sons of want
  Exhaustless riches find;
Riches above what earth can grant,
  And lasting as the mind.

Here the Redeemer's welcome voice
  Spreads heavenly peace around;
And life and everlasting joys
  Attend the blissful sound.

Oh! may these heavenly pages be
  My ever dear delight;
And still new beauties may I see,
  And still increasing light!

Divine Instructor, gracious Lord,
  Be Thou for ever near;
Teach me to love Thy sacred Word,
  And view my Saviour there.

A. Steele.

306.

COME, O Thou Traveller Unknown,
　　Whom still I hold, but cannot see,
My company before is gone,
　　And I am left alone with Thee:
With Thee all night I mean to stay,
And wrestle till the break of day.

Wilt Thou not yet to me reveal
　　Thy new, unutterable Name?
Tell me, I still beseech Thee, tell!
　　To know it now resolved I am:
Wrestling, I will not let Thee go,
Till I Thy Name, Thy Nature know.

Yield to me now, for I am weak,
　　But confident in self-despair;
Speak to my heart, in blessings speak,
　　Be conquered by my instant prayer;
Speak, or Thou never hence shalt move,
And tell me if Thy Name is Love.

My prayer hath power with God; the grace
　　Unspeakable I now receive;
Through faith I see Thee face to face,
　　I see Thee face to face, and live;
In vain I have not wept and strove;
Thy Nature, and Thy Name is Love.

I know Thee, Saviour, Who Thou art;
　　Jesus, the feeble sinner's Friend;
Nor wilt Thou with the night depart,
　　But stay, and love me to the end:
Thy mercies never shall remove;
Thy Nature, and Thy Name, is Love.

C. Wesley.

307.

THOU hidden Love of God, Whose height,
  Whose depth unfathomed no man knows,
I see from far Thy beauteous light,
  Inly I sigh for Thy repose:
My heart is pained, nor let it be
At rest, till it finds rest in Thee.

Is there a thing beneath the sun
  That strives with Thee my heart to share?
Oh! tear it thence, and reign alone,
  The Lord of every motion there:
Then shall my heart from earth be free,
When it has found repose in Thee.

Oh! hide this self from me, that I
  No more, but Christ in me may live!
My vile affections crucify,
  Nor let one darling lust survive:
In all things nothing may I see,
Nothing desire, or seek, but Thee.

O Love, Thy sovereign aid impart,
  To save me from forbidden care;
Chase this self-will through all my heart,
  Through all its latent mazes there:
Make me Thy duteous child, that I
Ceaseless may "Abba, Father" cry.

Each moment draw from earth away
  My heart that lowly waits Thy call;
Speak to my inmost soul, and say,
  "I am thy Life, thy God, thy All."
To feel Thy power, to hear Thy voice,
To taste Thy love, be all my choice!

J. Wesley.
(Translation from the German
of G. Tersteegen).

308.

LOVE Divine, all love excelling,
  Joy of heaven, to earth come down;
Fix in us Thy humble dwelling,
  All Thy faithful mercies crown;
Jesu, Thou art all Compassion,
  Pure, unbounded Love Thou art;
Visit us with Thy salvation,
  Enter every longing heart.

Come, Almighty to deliver,
  Let us all Thy life receive;
Suddenly return, and never,
  Never more Thy temples leave;
Thee we would be always blessing,
  Serve Thee as Thine hosts above;
Pray, and praise Thee without ceasing,
  Glory in Thy boundless love.

Finish then Thy new creation,
  Pure, unspotted may we be;
Let us see Thy great salvation
  Perfectly restored in Thee;
Changed from glory into glory,
  Till in heaven we take our place,
Till we cast our crowns before Thee,
  Lost in wonder, love, and praise.

C. Wesley.

309.

O THOU from Whom all goodness flows,
　I lift my heart to Thee;
In all my sorrows, conflicts, woes,
　Dear Lord, remember me!

When on my aching burdened heart
　My sins lie heavily,
Thy pardon grant, Thy peace impart,
　In love remember me!

When trials sore obstruct my way,
　And ills I cannot flee,
Oh! let my strength be as my day;
　For good remember me!

If on my face, for Thy dear Name,
　Shame and reproach shall be,
All hail reproach, and welcome shame,
　If Thou remember me!

And oh! when in the hour of death
　I wait Thy just decree,
Be this the prayer of my last breath,
　"Dear Lord, remember me!"

　　　　　　　　　　T. Haweis.

310.

JESU, Lover of my soul,
  Let me to Thy bosom fly,
While the nearer waters roll,
  While the tempest still is high;
Hide me, O my Saviour, hide,
  Till the storm of life be past;
Safe into the haven guide;
  O receive my soul at last.

Other refuge have I none;
  Hangs my helpless soul on Thee;
Leave, O leave me not alone,
  Still support and comfort me;
All my trust on Thee is stayed,
  All my help from Thee I bring:
Cover my defenceless head
  With the shadow of Thy wing.

Thou, O Christ, art all I want;
  More than all in Thee I find;
Raise the fallen, cheer the faint,
  Heal the sick, and lead the blind:
Thou of life the Fountain art;
  Freely let me take of Thee,
Spring Thou up within my heart,
  Rise to all Eternity.

C. Wesley.

311.

WEARY of earth, and laden with my sin,
　　I look at heaven and long to enter in;
But there no evil thing may find a home:
And yet I hear a Voice that bids me come.

So vile I am, how dare I hope to stand
In the pure glory of that holy land,
Before the whiteness of that throne appear?
Yet there are Hands stretched out to draw me near.

The while I fain would tread the heavenly way,
Evil is ever with me day by day;
Yet on mine ears the gracious tidings fall,
"Repent, confess, thou shalt be loosed from all."

It is the Voice of Jesus that I hear,
His are the Hands stretched out to draw me near,
And His the Blood that can for all atone,
And set me faultless there before the throne.

O great Absolver, grant my soul may wear
The lowliest garb of penitence and prayer,
That in the Father's courts my glorious dress
May be the garment of Thy righteousness.

Yea, Thou wilt answer for me, righteous Lord,
Thine all the merits, mine the great reward;
Thine the sharp thorns, and mine the golden crown,
Mine the life won, and Thine the life laid down.

Nought can I bring, dear Lord, for all I owe,
Yet let my full heart what it can bestow;
Like Mary's gift let my devotion prove,
Forgiven greatly, how I greatly love.

S. J. Stone.

312.

"COME unto Me, ye weary,
    And I will give you rest."
O blessèd voice of Jesus,
    Which comes to hearts opprest!
It tells of benediction,
    Of pardon, grace, and peace,
Of joy that hath no ending,
    Of love which cannot cease.

"Come unto Me, ye wanderers,
    And I will give you light."
O loving voice of Jesus,
    Which comes to cheer the night!
Our hearts were filled with sadness,
    And we had lost our way;
But He has brought us gladness
    And songs at break of day.

"Come unto Me, ye fainting,
    And I will give you life."
O cheering voice of Jesus,
    Which comes to aid our strife!
The foe is stern and eager,
    The fight is fierce and long;
But He has made us mighty,
    And stronger than the strong.

"And whosoever cometh,
    I will not cast him out."
O welcome voice of Jesus,
    Which drives away our doubt;
Which calls us very sinners,
    Unworthy though we be
Of love so free and boundless,
    To come, dear Lord, to Thee!

W. C. Dix.

313.

I HEARD the voice of Jesus say,
  " Come unto Me, and rest;
Lay down, thou weary one, lay down
  Thy head upon My breast."
I came to Jesus as I was,
  Weary, and worn, and sad;
I found in Him a resting-place,
  And He has made me glad.

I heard the voice of Jesus say,
  " Behold, I freely give
The living water; thirsty one,
  Stoop down, and drink, and live."
I came to Jesus, and I drank
  Of that life-giving stream;
My thirst was quenched, my soul revived,
  And now I live in Him.

I heard the voice of Jesus say,
  " I am this dark world's Light;
Look unto Me, thy morn shall rise,
  And all thy day be bright."
I looked to Jesus, and I found
  In Him my Star, my Sun;
And in that Light of Life I'll walk
  Till travelling days are done.

H. Bonar.

314.

HARK! my soul, it is the Lord;
    'Tis thy Saviour, hear His word;
Jesus speaks, and speaks to thee,
"Say, poor sinner, lov'st thou Me?

"I delivered thee when bound,
And, when bleeding, healed thy wound;
Sought thee wandering, set thee right,
Turned thy darkness into light.

"Can a woman's tender care
Cease towards the child she bare?
Yea, she may forgetful be,
Yet will I remember thee.

"Mine is an unchanging love,
Higher than the heights above,
Deeper than the depths beneath,
Free and faithful, strong as death.

"Thou shalt see My glory soon,
When the work of grace is done;
Partner of My throne shall be;
Say, poor sinner, lov'st thou Me?"

Lord, it is my chief complaint
That my love is weak and faint,
Yet I love Thee, and adore;
Oh! for grace to love Thee more!

W. Cowper.

315.

LEAD, kindly Light, amid the encircling gloom,
Lead Thou me on!
The night is dark, and I am far from home,
Lead Thou me on!
Keep Thou my feet; I do not ask to see
The distant scene—one step enough for me.

I was not ever thus, nor prayed that Thou
Should'st lead me on:
I loved to choose and see my path, but now
Lead Thou me on!
I loved the garish day, and, spite of fears,
Pride ruled my will: remember not past years.

So long Thy power hath blest me, sure it still
Will lead me on,
O'er moor and fen, o'er crag and torrent, till
The night is gone;
And with the morn those angel faces smile
Which I have loved long since, and lost awhile.

Cardinal Newman.

316.

JESU dulcis memoria,
    Dans vera cordi gaudia,
Sed super mel et omnia
Ejus dulcis praesentia.

Nil canitur suävius,
Nil auditur jucundius,
Nil cogitatur dulcius,
Quam Jesus Dei Filius.

Jesu, spes paenitentibus,
Quam pius es petentibus!
Quam bonus Te quaerentibus!
Sed quid invenientibus?

Jesu, dulcedo cordium,
Fons veri, lumen mentium,
Excedens omne gaudium,
Et omne desiderium.

Nec lingua valet dicere
Nec litera exprimere,
Expertus potest credere,
Quid sit Jesum diligere.

Saint Bernard of Clairvaux.

317.

JESU, the very thought of Thee
  With sweetness fills the breast;
But sweeter far Thy face to see,
  And in Thy presence rest.

Tongue never spake, ear never heard,
  Nor e'er from heart o'erflowed
A dearer name, a sweeter word,
  Than Jesus, Son of God.

O Hope of every contrite heart,
  O Joy of all the meek,
To those who fall how kind Thou art!
  How good to those who seek!

But what to those who find? Ah! this
  No tongue nor pen can show:
The love of Jesus, what it is,
  None but His loved ones know.

Jesu, our only Joy be Thou,
  As Thou our Prize wilt be:
In Thee be all our glory now,
  And through Eternity!

E. Caswall.

318.

CHILDREN of the Heavenly King,
　　As ye journey, sweetly sing;
Sing your Saviour's worthy praise,
Glorious in His works and ways.

We are travelling home to God,
In the way the fathers trod:
They are happy now, and we
Soon their happiness shall see.

Lift your eyes, ye sons of light!
Zion's city is in sight:
There our endless home shall be,
There our Lord we soon shall see.

Fear not, brethren, joyful stand
On the borders of your land;
Christ, the Everlasting Son,
Bids you undismayed go on.

Lord, obediently we go,
Gladly leaving all below:
Only Thou our Leader be,
And we still will follow Thee.

J. Cennick.

319.

FROM Egypt's bondage come,
   Where death and darkness reign,
We seek a new, a better home,
   Where we our rest shall gain.
      Alleluia!
   We are on our way to God.

There sin and sorrow cease,
   And, every conflict o'er,
There we shall dwell in endless peace,
   And never hunger more.
      Alleluia!
   We are on our way to God.

There in celestial strains
   Enraptured myriads sing;
And love in every bosom reigns,
   For God Himself is King.
      Alleluia!
   We are on our way to God.

We soon shall join the throng,
   And soon their pleasures share;
And sing the everlasting song,
   With all the ransomed there.
      Alleluia!
   We are on our way to God.

T. Kelly.

320.

WHERE'ER have trod Thy sacred feet,
  Teach us, O Lord, Thy steps to trace,
Where men in busy concourse meet,
  Or in the lonely wilderness.

Bid us with Thee to watch and pray,
  With Thee to die, with Thee to rise,
With Thee to bear our cross each day,
  With Thee to soar beyond the skies.

Where'er Thou art may we remain,
  Where'er Thou goest may we go :
With Thee, O Lord, no grief is pain ;
  Away from Thee, all joy is woe.

Oh! may we in each holy tide,
  Each solemn season, dwell with Thee,
Content if only by Thy side,
  In life or death, we still may be!

321.

LORD, as to Thy dear Cross we flee,
   And plead to be forgiven,
So let Thy life our pattern be,
   And form our souls for heaven.

Help us, through good report and ill,
   Our daily cross to bear;
Like Thee to do our Father's Will,
   Our brethren's griefs to share.

Let grace our selfishness expel,
   Our earthliness refine,
And kindness in our bosoms dwell,
   As free and true as Thine.

If joy shall at Thy bidding fly,
   And grief's dark day come on,
We in our turn would meekly cry
   " Father, Thy Will be done!"

Kept peaceful in the midst of strife,
   Forgiving and forgiven,
Oh! may we lead the pilgrim's life,
   And follow Thee to heaven!

J. H. Gurney.

322.

"COME to a desert place apart,
　　And rest a little while."
So spake the Lord, when limbs and heart
　　Waxed faint and sick through toil.

High communings with God He sought;
　　But, where He sought them, found
The restless crowd together brought,
　　And labour's weary round.

Then not a thought to self was given,
　　Nor breathed He word of blame:
He fed their souls with bread from heaven,
　　Then stayed their sinking frame.

Turned He, when that long task was done,
　　To sleep fatigue away?
When on the desert sank the sun,
　　The Saviour waked to pray.

O perfect Pattern from above,
　　So strengthen us, that ne'er
Prayer keep us back from works of love,
　　Nor works of love from prayer.

J. Anstice.

323.

O HOLY Saviour, Friend unseen,
    Since on Thine arm Thou bidd'st us lean,
Help us throughout life's changing scene
      To cling to Thee.

Blest with this fellowship divine,
Take what Thou wilt, we'll not repine;
For, as the branches to the vine,
      We cling to Thee.

Though far from home, way-worn, opprest,
Here we have found a place of rest;
As exiles still, yet not unblest,
      We cling to Thee.

What though the world deceitful prove,
And earthly friends and hopes remove?
With patient uncomplaining love
      We cling to Thee.

Though oft we seem to tread alone
Life's dreary waste with thorns o'ergrown,
Thy voice of love in gentlest tone
      Cries " Cling to Me."

Blest is our lot, whate'er befall;
No foes can harm, no fears appal,
Since as our Strength, our Rock, our All,
      We cling to Thee.

C. Elliott.

324.

BLEST be Thy love, dear Lord,
　That taught us this sweet way,
Only to love Thee for Thyself,
　And for that love obey.

O Thou, our souls' chief hope,
　We to Thy mercy fly:
Where'er we are, Thou canst protect,
　Whate'er we need supply.

Whether we sleep or wake,
　To Thee we both resign:
By night we see, as well as day,
　If Thy light on us shine.

Whether we live or die,
　Both we submit to Thee:
In death we live, as well as life,
　If Thine in death we be.

J. Austin.

325.

HOW sweet the Name of Jesus sounds
    In a believer's ear!
It soothes his sorrows, heals his wounds,
    And drives away his fear.

It makes the wounded spirit whole,
    And calms the troubled breast;
'Tis manna to the hungry soul,
    And to the weary rest.

Dear Name, the rock on which I build,
    My shield and hiding-place,
My never-failing treasury, filled
    With boundless stores of grace!

Jesus, my Master, Shepherd, Friend,
    My Prophet, Priest, and King,
My Lord, my Life, my Way, my End,
    Accept the praise I bring.

Weak is the effort of my heart,
    And cold my warmest thought;
But, when I see Thee as Thou art,
    I'll praise Thee as I ought.

Till then I would Thy love proclaim
    With every fleeting breath;
And may the music of Thy Name
    Refresh my soul in death!

J. Newton.

326.

GLORIOUS things of thee are spoken,
   Zion, city of our God:
He Whose word cannot be broken
   Formed thee for His own abode:
On the Rock of Ages founded,
   What can shake thy sure repose?
With Salvation's wall surrounded,
   Thou may'st smile at all thy foes.

Though the world esteem thee lowly,
   Though they pass thy ramparts by,
Yet the Lord, Whose Name is holy,
   He Who fills Eternity,
He Whom not the heaven containeth,
   Not the high and holy place,
Still within thy walls remaineth,
   Still upholds thee with His grace.

Heed not thou reproach and scorning,
   Fear not threats or danger near;
Soon shall rise the blissful morning
   When the Bridegroom shall appear:
Then, His light abiding in thee,
   Who so glad, so blest as thou?
Happy they that dwell within thee,
   They that love and own thee now!

J. Newton.

327.

COME, let us join our cheerful songs
 With angels round the Throne;
Ten thousand thousand are their tongues,
 But all their joys are one.

"Worthy the Lamb that died," they cry,
 "To be exalted thus."
"Worthy the Lamb," our lips reply,
 "For He was slain for us."

Jesus is worthy to receive
 Honour and power divine;
And blessings more than we can give
 Be, Lord, for ever Thine.

Let all Creation join in one,
 To bless the sacred Name
Of Him that sits upon the Throne,
 And to adore the Lamb.

I. Watts.

328.

YE servants of God, your Master proclaim,
  And publish abroad His wonderful Name;
The Name all-victorious of Jesus extol;
His kingdom is glorious, and rules over all.

God ruleth on high, Almighty to save;
And still He is nigh, His presence we have;
The great congregation His triumph shall sing,
Ascribing salvation to Jesus our King.

"Salvation to God, Who sits on the Throne!"
Let all cry aloud, and honour the Son;
Our Saviour's great praises the angels proclaim,
Fall down on their faces, and worship the Lamb.

Then let us adore, and give Him His right,
All glory and power, all wisdom and might,
All honour and blessing, with angels above,
And thanks never-ceasing for infinite love.

C. Wesley.

329.

WE love the place, O God,
　　Wherein Thine honour dwells ;
The joy of Thine abode
　　All earthly joy excels.

It is the House of Prayer,
　　Wherein Thy servants meet ;
And Thou, O Lord, art there
　　Thy chosen flock to greet.

We love Thy Table, Lord,
　　Oh, what on earth so dear?
For there, in faith adored,
　　We find Thy Presence near.

We love the Word of Life,
　　The Word that tells of peace,
Of comfort in the strife,
　　And joys that never cease.

We love to sing below
　　For mercies freely given ;
But oh ! we long to know
　　The triumph-song of heaven.

Lord Jesus, give us grace
　　On earth to love Thee more,
In heaven to see Thy face,
　　And with Thy saints adore.

Dean Bullock and Sir H. W. Baker.

330.

PLEASANT are Thy courts above
   In the land of light and love;
Pleasant are Thy courts below
In this land of sin and woe:
Oh! my spirit longs and faints
For the converse of Thy saints,
For the brightness of Thy face,
For Thy fulness, God of grace.

Happy birds that sing and fly
Round Thine altars, O Most High!
Happier souls that find a rest
In a Heavenly Father's breast!
Like the wandering dove that found
No repose on earth around,
They can to their ark repair,
And enjoy it ever there.

Happy souls! their praises flow
Even in this vale of woe;
Waters in the desert rise,
Manna feeds them from the skies;
On they go from strength to strength,
Till they reach Thy throne at length,
At Thy feet adoring fall,
Who hast led them safe through all.

Lord, be mine this prize to win,
Guide me through a world of sin;
Keep me by Thy saving grace,
Give me at Thy side a place:
Sun and Shield alike Thou art;
Guide and guard my erring heart;
Grace and glory flow from Thee;
Shower, O shower them, Lord, on me.

H. F. Lyte.

331.

O GOD of Hosts, the mighty Lord,
　　How lovely is the place
Where Thou, enthroned in glory, show'st
　　The brightness of Thy face!

My longing soul faints with desire
　　To view Thy blest abode;
My panting heart and flesh cry out
　　For Thee, the living God.

O Lord of Hosts, my King and God,
　　How highly blest are they
Who in Thy temple always dwell,
　　And there Thy praise display!

Thrice happy they whose choice has Thee
　　Their sure protection made;
Who long to tread the sacred ways
　　That to Thy dwelling lead!

Thus they proceed from strength to strength,
　　And still approach more near,
Till all on Zion's holy mount
　　Before their God appear.

N. Tate and N. Brady.

332.

"LIFT up your hearts!" We lift them, Lord, to Thee;
Here, at Thy feet, none other may we see:
"Lift up your hearts!" E'en so, with one accord,
We lift them up, we lift them to the Lord.

Above the level of the former years,
The mire of sin, the slough of guilty fears,
The mist of doubt, the blight of love's decay,
O Lord of Light, lift all our hearts to-day.

Above the swamps of subterfuge and shame,
The deeds, the thoughts, that honour may not name,
The halting tongue that dares not tell the whole,
O Lord of Truth, lift every Christian soul.

Above the storms that vex this lower state,
Pride, jealousy, and envy, rage, and hate,
And cold mistrust that holds e'en friends apart,
O Lord of Love, lift every brother's heart.

Lift us to Thee, each boy, each master here,
Our friends, our homes, and all we count most dear;
Learning, and wit, grace, vigour, childish glee,
Lift them, O Lord, and lift them all to Thee.

Lift every gift that Thou Thyself hast given;
Low lies the best till lifted up to heaven:
Low lie the bounding heart, the teeming brain,
Till, sent from God, they mount to God again.

Then, as the trumpet-call, in after years,
"Lift up your hearts!" rings pealing in our ears,
Still shall those hearts respond, with full accord,
"We lift them up, we lift them to the Lord."

H. M. Butler.

333.

ONWARD, holy champion!
 Run the Christian race;
Leave the world behind thee,
 Heavenward set thy face;
Fresh from cleansing water,
 Bright with oil divine,
Strong with healthiest nurture,
 Living Bread and Wine!

Onward, holy champion!
 Lay all weight aside,
All enfeebling pleasure,
 All encumbering pride;
Shun the subtle pitfalls
 Framed by Satan's spite;
Let no smiles allure thee,
 Let no frowns affright!

Onward, holy champion!
 Angels beaming down
Watch thy brave endeavour,
 Weave thy future crown;
Christ, thy mighty Saviour,
 Helps thy striving soul,
And thy prize awaits thee
 At the heavenly goal.

334.

JERUSALEM, Jerusalem,
  Enthronèd once on high,
Thou favoured home of God on earth,
  Thou heaven below the sky!
Now brought to bondage with thy sons,
  A curse and grief to see,
Jerusalem, Jerusalem,
  Our tears shall flow for thee.

Oh! hadst thou known thy day of grace,
  And flocked beneath the wing
Of Him who called thee lovingly,
  Thine own Anointed King!
But now thy day is sunk in night,
  Thy time of mercy spent;
For heavy was thy children's crime,
  And strange its punishment.

Oh! gaze not idly on their fall,
  But, sinner, warnèd be!
Who sparèd not His chosen seed
  May send His wrath on thee.
Their day of grace is sunk in night,
  Thy noon is in its prime:
Oh! turn, and seek thy Saviour's face,
  In this accepted time!

Bishop Heber.

335.

MAKE haste, my soul, to live;
　　Soon comes the hour to die:
Time hurries past thee like the breeze;
　　How swift its moments fly!

To breathe and wake and sleep,
　　To smile, to sigh, to grieve,
To move in idleness through earth,
　　This, this is not to live.

Make haste, my soul, to do
　　Whatever must be done;
Thou hast no time to lose in sloth,
　　Thy day will soon be gone.

Up then with speed, and work;
　　Fling ease and self away:
This is no time for thee to sleep;
　　Up, watch and work and pray.

The useful, not the great,
　　The thing that never dies,
The silent toil that is not lost,
　　Set these before thine eyes.

Make haste, my soul, to live;
　　Thy time is almost o'er:
Oh! sleep not, dream not, but arise;
　　The Judge is at the door.

H. Bonar.

336.

TEACH me to live; 'tis easier far to die,
  Gently and silently to pass away;
On earth's long night to close the heavy eye,
  And waken to the realms of glorious day.

Teach me that harder lesson, how to live,
  To serve Thee in the darkest paths of life:
Arm me for conflict now; fresh vigour give,
  And make me more than conqueror in the strife.

Teach me to live; no idler let me be,
  But in Thy service hand and heart employ,
Prepared to do Thy bidding cheerfully;
  Be this my highest and my holiest joy.

Teach me to live, my daily cross to bear,
  Nor murmur though I bend beneath its load:
Only be with me, let me feel Thee near;
  Thy smile sheds gladness on the darkest road.

Teach me to live, with kindly words for all,
  Wearing no cold repulsive brow of gloom,
Waiting with cheerful patience, till Thy call
  Summons my spirit to her heavenly home.

337.

LORD, Thy mercy now entreating,
  Low before Thy throne we fall,
Our misdeeds to Thee confessing,
  On Thy Name we humbly call.

Sinful thoughts, and words unloving,
  Rise against us one by one;
Acts unworthy, deeds unthinking,
  Good that we have left undone;

Hearts that far from Thee were straying,
  While in prayer we bowed the knee;
Lips that, while Thy praises sounding,
  Lifted not the voice to Thee;

Precious moments idly wasted,
  Precious hours in folly spent;
Christian vow and fight unheeded,
  Scarce a thought to wisdom lent.

Lord, Thy mercy still entreating,
  We with shame our sins would own;
From henceforth, the time redeeming,
  May we live to Thee alone.

Heavenly Father, bless Thy children;
  Hearken from Thy throne on high;
Loving Saviour, Holy Spirit,
  Hear and heed our humble cry.

338.

WE ask for life, and mean thereby
   A few uncertain years,
The sunshine of a changeful sky
   Over a vale of tears;
But Thou art better than our prayers,
   And givest, in Thy love,
A shorter path through earthly cares,
   A longer rest above.

We ask for life, Thy work to do,
   For Thee to toil and win,
To warn the many, save the few,
   From sorrow and from sin;
In rolling years and fleeting breath
   We think the boon must lie:
Thou teachest that a faithful death
   Is highest victory.

J. S. B. Monsell.

339.

PRAYER is the soul's sincere desire,
   Uttered or unexpressed;
The motion of a hidden fire,
   That trembles in the breast.

Prayer is the burden of a sigh,
   The falling of a tear,
The upward glancing of an eye
   When none but God is near.

Prayer is the simplest form of speech
   That infant-lips can try;
Prayer, the sublimest strains that reach
   The Majesty on high.

Prayer is the Christian's vital breath,
   The Christian's native air,
His watchword at the gates of death;
   He enters heaven with prayer.

Prayer is the contrite sinner's voice,
   Returning from his ways,
While angels in their songs rejoice,
   And cry, "Behold, he prays!"

O Thou, by Whom we come to God,
   The Life, the Truth, the Way,
The path of prayer Thyself hast trod;
   Lord, teach us how to pray.

J. Montgomery.

340.

"ASK, and ye surely shall receive;"
   Yea, Lord, we trust Thy word;
We lift our voice, and we believe
   That we are surely heard.

We ask not anything that earth
   Can give or take away;
Thou, Who hast kept us from our birth,
   Wilt guard us day by day.

We ask for light and love and strength
   All selfish snares to shun:
We ask that we may ask at length,
   "Thy Will, not ours, be done!"

We ask that to each separate heart
   Of all our brethren here
Thy one best gift Thou wouldst impart,
   The wisdom of Thy fear.

May young and old conspire to prize,
   And labour to secure,
Whatever things are true, and wise,
   Noble, and just, and pure.

O Thou, by Whom we come to God,
   The Life, the Truth, the Way,
The path of prayer Thyself hast trod;
   Lord, teach us how to pray.

H. M. Butler and J. Montgomery.

341.

OH! for a closer walk with God,
  A calm and heavenly frame,
A light to shine upon the road
  That leads me to the Lamb!

Return, O Holy Dove, return,
  Sweet messenger of rest;
I hate the sins that made Thee mourn,
  And drove Thee from my breast.

The dearest idol I have known,
  Whate'er that idol be,
Help me to tear it from Thy throne,
  And worship only Thee.

So shall my walk be close with God,
  Calm and serene my frame;
So purer light shall mark the road
  That leads me to the Lamb.

W. Cowper.

342.

OH! for a heart to praise my God,
  A heart from guilt set free,
A heart that's sprinkled with the blood
  So freely shed for me!

A heart resigned, submissive, meek,
  My blest Redeemer's throne;
Where only Christ is heard to speak,
  Where Jesus reigns alone!

A humble, lowly, contrite heart,
  Believing, true and clean;
Which neither life nor death can part
  From Him Who dwells within!

A heart in every thought renewed,
  And filled with love divine;
Perfect and right, and pure, and good,
  A copy, Lord, of Thine!

Thy Nature, gracious Lord, impart,
  Come quickly from above;
Write Thy new Name upon my heart,
  Thy new best Name of Love.

C. Wesley.

343.

GO when the morning shineth,
  Go when the noon is bright,
Go when the eve declineth,
  Go in the hush of night:
Go with pure mind and feeling,
  Fling earthly thoughts away,
And, in thy chamber kneeling,
  Do thou in secret pray.

Remember all who love thee,
  All who are loved by thee;
Pray too for those that hate thee,
  If any such there be:
Then for thyself in meekness
  A blessing humbly claim,
And link with each petition
  Thy great Redeemer's Name.

But if 'tis e'er denied thee
  In solitude to pray;
Should holy thoughts come o'er thee
  When friends are round thy way;
E'en then in silent worship
  Thy spirit raised above
Shall reach His throne of glory,
  Of mercy, truth and love.

Oh! not a joy or blessing
  With this can we compare,
The power that He hath given us
  To pour our souls in prayer.
Whene'er thou pin'st in sadness,
  Before His footstool fall;
Remember in thy gladness
  His Love Who gave thee all.

                              J. C. Simpson.

344.

LORD, not for store of worldly wealth,
  Nor worldly fame, we pray,
Nor worldly joys, which brightly bloom,
  And quickly fade away.

Not to the world, nor to ourselves,
  But to Thy holy eyes
We look; O give us godly fear,
  O make us meekly wise!

True wisdom, while it gives, receives;
  By scattering gets increase;
And all her ways are pleasantness,
  And all her paths are peace.

Honour and wealth are in her hand,
  True glory she bestows;
A holy stream of life and joy
  From her pure well-spring flows.

                    Bishop Christopher Wordsworth.

345.

MY God, my Father, while I stray
    Far from my home, on life's rough way,
O teach me from my heart to say,
      Thy Will be done!

Though dark my path and sad my lot,
Let me be still, and murmur not,
Or breathe the prayer divinely taught,
      Thy Will be done!

If Thou shouldst call me to resign
What most I prize, it ne'er was mine;
I only yield Thee what was Thine;
      Thy Will be done!

If but my fainting heart be blest
With Thy sweet Spirit for its guest,
My God, to Thee I leave the rest;
      Thy Will be done!

Renew my will from day to day;
Blend it with Thine, and take away
All that now makes it hard to say,
      Thy Will be done!

Then, when on earth I breathe no more,
The prayer, oft mixed with tears before,
I'll sing upon a happier shore,
      Thy Will be done!

C. Elliott.

346.

ETERNAL God, we look to Thee,
   To Thee for help we fly:
Thine eye alone our wants can see,
   Thy hand alone supply.

Lord, let Thy fear within us dwell,
   Thy love our footsteps guide:
That love will all vain love expel;
   That fear, all fear beside.

Not what we wish, but what we want,
   Oh! let Thy grace supply:
The good, unasked, in mercy grant;
   The ill, though asked, deny.

J. Merrick.

347.

FATHER, whate'er of earthly bliss
   Thy sovereign Will denies,
Accepted at Thy throne of grace
   Let this petition rise.

Give me a calm and thankful heart,
   From every murmur free;
The blessings of Thy grace impart,
   And make me live to Thee.

Let the sweet hope that Thou art mine
   My life and death attend;
Thy Presence through my journey shine,
   And crown my journey's end.

A. Steele.

348.

THERE is a land of pure delight,
　　Where saints immortal reign;
Eternal day excludes the night,
　　And pleasures banish pain.

There everlasting spring abides,
　　And never-withering flowers:
Death, like a narrow sea, divides
　　This heavenly land from ours.

Sweet fields beyond the swelling flood
　　Stand dressed in living green:
So to the Jews old Canaan stood,
　　While Jordan rolled between.

But timorous mortals start and shrink
　　To cross this narrow sea,
And linger shivering on the brink,
　　And fear to launch away.

Oh! could we make our doubts remove,
　　Those gloomy doubts that rise,
And see the Canaan that we love
　　With unbeclouded eyes;

Could we but climb where Moses stood,
　　And view the landscape o'er,
Not Jordan's stream, nor death's cold flood,
　　Should fright us from the shore.

I. Watts.

349.

LET us with a gladsome mind
    Praise the Lord, for He is kind!
Long our island throne has stood,
Planted on the ocean flood;
Crowned with rock, and girt with sea,
Home and refuge of the free:
For His mercies aye endure,
Ever faithful, ever sure.

On that island throne have sate
Alfred's goodness, Edward's state;
Princely strength and queenly grace,
Lengthened line of royal race:
Round that throne have stood of old
Seers and statesmen, firm and bold;
Burghley's wisdom, Hampden's fire,
Chatham's force in son and sire.

Let us with a gladsome mind
Praise the Lord, for He is kind!
Him, in homely English tongue,
Epic lay and lyric song,
Shakespeare's myriad-minded verse,
Milton's heavenward strains, rehearse:
For His mercies aye endure,
Ever faithful, ever sure.

Let us with a gladsome mind
Praise the Lord, for He is kind!
Soldiers tried in every clime,
Sailors famous through all time,
Hands of iron, hearts of oak,
Fresh from their Creator's stroke,
These His gifts for aye endure,
Ever faithful, ever sure.

Science, with her thousand eyes,
Sunless mine and starlit skies
Probes and pierces far and near,
Man's estate to guide and cheer:
Hither, in our heathen night,
Came of yore the Gospel light;
By the Saviour's sacred story
"Angles" turned to angels' glory.

Let us with a gladsome mind
Praise the Lord, for He is kind!
Rustic churchyard, lordly pile,
Studious cloister, crowded aisle,
Lady-chapel, gorgeous shrine,
All proclaim with voice divine
That Thy mercies still endure,
Ever faithful, ever sure.

Let us with a gladsome mind
Praise the Lord, for He is kind!
Breaking with a gracious hand
Ancient error's subtle band;
Opening wide the sacred page
Kindling hope in saint and sage.
For His mercies aye endure,
Ever faithful, ever sure.

Give us homes serene and pure,
Settled freedom, laws secure;
Truthful lips and minds sincere,
Faith and love that cast out fear:
Grant that Light and Life divine
Long on England's shores may shine;
Grant that People, Church and Throne
May in all good deeds be one.

Dean Stanley.

350.

LORD, we thank Thee for the pleasure
    That our happy lifetime gives,
The inestimable treasure
    Of a soul that ever lives;
Mind that looks before and after,
    Yearning for its home above,
Human tears, and human laughter,
    And the depth of human love:

For the thrill, the leap, the gladness
    Of our pulses flowing free;
E'en for every touch of sadness
    That may bring us nearer Thee:
But, above all other kindness,
    Thine unutterable love,
Which, to heal our sin and blindness,
    Sent Thy dear Son from above.

Teach us so our days to number
    That we may be early wise;
Dreamy mist, or cloud of slumber
    Never dull our heavenward eyes:
Hearty be our work, and willing,
    As to Thee, and not to men;
For we know our soul's fulfilling
    Is in heaven, not till then.

Dean Jex Blake.

351.

PRAISE to the Lord! the Almighty, the King of
    Creation!
O my soul, praise Him, for He is thy health and salvation!
        All ye who hear,
        Now to His temple draw near,
    Join me in glad adoration.

Praise to the Lord! Who o'er all things so wondrously
    reigneth,
Shelters thee under His wings, yea so gently sustaineth:
        Hast thou not seen
        How thy desires have been
    Granted in what He ordaineth?

Praise to the Lord! Who doth prosper thy work and
    defend thee;
Surely His goodness and mercy here daily attend thee:
        Ponder anew
        What the Almighty can do,
    If with His love He befriend thee.

Praise to the Lord! Oh! let all that is in me adore Him!
All that hath life and breath, come now with praises
    before Him!
        Let the Amen
        Sound from His people again;
    Gladly for aye we adore Him.

C. Winkworth.
(Translation from the German
of J. Neander).

352.

SONGS of praise the angels sang,
  Heaven with Alleluias rang,
When Jehovah's work begun,
When He spake, and it was done.

Songs of praise awoke the morn
When the Prince of Peace was born;
Songs of praise arose when He
Captive led captivity.

Heaven and earth must pass away,
Songs of praise shall crown that day;
God will make new heavens and earth;
Songs of praise shall hail their birth.

And shall man alone be dumb
Till that glorious Kingdom come?
No! the Church delights to raise
Psalms, and hymns, and songs of praise.

Saints below, with heart and voice,
Now in songs of praise rejoice,
Learning here, by faith and love,
Songs of praise to sing above.

Borne upon their latest breath
Songs of praise shall conquer death;
Then, amidst eternal joy,
Songs of praise their powers employ.

J. Montgomery.

353.

PRAISE, my soul, the King of Heaven!
  To His feet thy tribute bring:
Ransomed, healed, restored, forgiven,
  Who like thee His praise should sing?
    Praise Him! Praise Him!
  Praise the Everlasting King!

Praise Him for His grace and favour
  To our fathers in distress!
Praise Him still the same for ever,
  Slow to chide, and swift to bless!
    Praise Him! Praise Him!
  Glorious in His faithfulness!

Angels in the height, adore Him!
  Ye behold Him face to face;
Saints triumphant, bow before Him,
  Gathered in from every race:
    Praise Him! Praise Him!
  Praise with us the God of Grace!

H. F. Lyte.

354.

O GOD, our Father far above,
　　We praise Thy Name for all the love
　Thou in Thy Son dost give us;
In Him are we made one with Thee,
Our Brother and our Friend is He;
　Should aught affright or grieve us?
He is Greatest, Best, and Highest,
　　　　Ever nighest
　　　　To the weakest;
Fear no foes, if Him thou seekest.

Oh! praise to Him Who came to save,
Who conquered death and burst the grave!
　Each day new praise resoundeth
To Him the Lamb Who once was slain,
The Friend Whom none shall trust in vain,
　Whose grace for aye aboundeth:
Sing, ye heavens, tell the story
　　　　Of His glory,
　　　　Till His praises
Flood with light earth's darkest places.

Thou here our Comfort, there our Crown,
Thou King of Heaven, Who camest down
　To dwell as man beside us,
Our heart doth praise Thee o'er and o'er;
If Thou art mine, I ask no more,
　Be wealth or fame denied me;
Thee we follow; none who proves Thee,
　　　　None who loves Thee
　　　　Finds Thee fail him;
Lord of life, Thy powers avail him.

C. Winkworth.
(*Translation from the German
of J. A. Schlegel*).

355.

GO up, go up, my heart!
    Dwell with thy God above;
For here thou canst not rest,
    Nor here give out thy love.

Go up, go up, my heart!
    Be not a trifler here;
Ascend above these clouds,
    Dwell in a higher sphere.

Let not thy love flow out
    To things so soiled and dim;
Go up to heaven and God,
    Take up thy love to Him.

Go up, reluctant heart!
    Take up thy rest above;
Arise, earth-clinging thoughts,
    Ascend, my lingering love.

                    H. Bonar.

356.

PRAISE the Lord! ye Heavens adore Him,
　　Praise Him, angels in the height!
Sun and moon, rejoice before Him,
　Praise Him, all ye stars and light!
Praise the Lord! for He hath spoken;
　Worlds His mighty voice obeyed;
Laws which never shall be broken
　For their guidance He has made.

Praise the Lord! for He is glorious;
　Never shall His promise fail:
God hath made His saints victorious,
　Sin and death shall not prevail.
Praise the God of our Salvation;
　Hosts on high, His power proclaim!
Heaven and earth and all creation,
　Laud and magnify His Name!

357.

L ORD, it belongs not to my care
    Whether I die or live;
To love and serve Thee is my share,
    And this Thy grace must give.

If life be long, oh! make me glad
    The longer to obey;
If short, no labourer is sad
    To end his toilsome day.

Christ leads me through no darker rooms
    Than He went through before;
He that unto God's kingdom comes
    Must enter by this door.

Come, Lord, when grace hath made me meet
    Thy blessèd face to see:
For if Thy work on earth be sweet,
    What will Thy glory be!

My knowledge of that life is small,
    The eye of faith is dim;
But 'tis enough that Christ knows all,
    And I shall be with Him.

R. Baxter.

358.

CHRIST is our corner-stone,
On Him alone we build;
With His true saints alone
The courts of heaven are filled:
On His great love
Our hopes we place
Of present grace
And joys above.

Oh! then with hymns of praise
These hallowed courts shall ring;
Our voices we will raise
The Three in One to sing;
And thus proclaim
In joyful song,
Both loud and long,
That glorious Name.

Here, gracious God, do Thou
For evermore draw nigh;
Accept each faithful vow,
And mark each suppliant sigh;
In copious shower
On all who pray
Each holy day
Thy blessings pour.

Here may we gain from heaven
The grace which we implore;
And may that grace, once given,
Be with us evermore,
Until that day
When all the blest
To endless rest
Are called away.

J. Chandler.
(Translation from the Latin).

359.

JESU, my Saviour, look on me,
 For I am weary and oppressed;
I come to cast myself on Thee;
  Thou art my Rest.

Look down on me, for I am weak;
I feel the toilsome journey's length;
Thine aid omnipotent I seek;
  Thou art my Strength.

I am bewildered on my way;
Dark and tempestuous is the night;
Oh! shed Thou forth some cheering ray;
  Thou art my Light.

When Satan flings his fiery darts,
I look to Thee; my terrors cease;
Thy Cross a hiding-place imparts;
  Thou art my Peace.

Standing alone on Jordan's brink,
In that tremendous latest strife,
Thou wilt not suffer me to sink;
  Thou art my Life.

Thou wilt my every want supply,
E'en to the end, whate'er befall;
Through life, in death, eternally,
  Thou art my All.

C. Elliott.

360.

JESU, Thou joy of loving hearts,
　　Thou Fount of life, Thou Light of men,
From the best bliss that earth imparts
We turn unfilled to Thee again.

Thy truth unchanged hath ever stood,
Thou savest those that on Thee call;
To them that seek Thee Thou art good;
To them that find Thee, All in all!

We taste Thee, O Thou living Bread,
And long to feast upon Thee still;
We drink of Thee, the Fountain-head,
And thirst our souls from Thee to fill.

Our restless spirits yearn for Thee,
Where'er our changeful lot is cast;
Glad when Thy gracious smile we see,
Blest when our faith can hold Thee fast.

O Jesu, ever with us stay;
Make all our moments calm and bright;
Chase the dark night of sin away;
Shed o'er the world Thy holy light.

R. Palmer.
(*Translation from the Latin
of Saint Bernard of Clairvaux*).

361.

THOU knowest, Lord, the weariness and sorrow
  Of the sad heart that comes to Thee for rest;
Cares of to-day, and burdens for to-morrow,
  Blessings implored, and sins to be confessed;
We come before Thee at Thy gracious word,
And lay them at Thy feet: Thou knowest, Lord.

Thou knowest all the past; how long and blindly
  On the dark mountains the lost wanderer strayed;
How the good Shepherd followed, and how kindly
  He bore it home, upon His shoulders laid;
And healed the bleeding wounds, and soothed the pain,
And brought back life and hope and strength again.

Thou knowest all the present; each temptation,
  Each toilsome duty, each foreboding fear;
All to each one assigned of tribulation,
  Or to belovèd ones, than self more dear;
All pensive memories, as we journey on,
Longings for vanished smiles and voices gone.

Thou knowest all the future; gleams of gladness
  By stormy clouds too quickly overcast;
Hours of sweet fellowship and parting sadness,
  And the dark river to be crossed at last.
Oh! what could hope and confidence afford
To tread that path but this, "Thou knowest, Lord"?

Thou knowest, not alone as God All-knowing,
  As Man our mortal weakness Thou hast proved:
On earth, with purest sympathies o'erflowing,
  O Saviour, Thou hast wept, and Thou hast loved;
And love and sorrow still to Thee may come,
And find a hiding-place, a rest, a home.

Therefore we come, Thy gentle call obeying,
  And lay our sins and sorrows at Thy feet;
On everlasting strength our weakness staying,
  Clothed in Thy robe of righteousness complete;
Then rising and refreshed we leave Thy throne,
And follow on to know as we are known.

362.

JESUS, Lord of Life and Glory,
  Bend from heaven Thy gracious ear;
While our waiting souls adore Thee,
  Friend of helpless sinners, hear:
    By Thy mercy,
  Oh! deliver us, good Lord!

From the depths of nature's blindness,
  From the hardening power of sin,
From all malice and unkindness,
  From the pride that lurks within,
    By Thy mercy,
  Oh! deliver us, good Lord!

When temptation sorely presses
  In the day of Satan's power,
In our time of deep distresses,
  In each dark and trying hour,
    By Thy mercy,
  Oh! deliver us, good Lord!

When the world around is smiling,
  In the time of wealth and ease,
Earthly joys our hearts beguiling,
  In the day of health and peace,
    By Thy mercy,
  Oh! deliver us, good Lord!

In the weary hours of sickness,
  In the time of grief and pain,
When we feel our mortal weakness,
  When the creature's help is vain,
    By Thy mercy,
  Oh! deliver us, good Lord!

In the solemn hour of dying,
  In the awful judgment day,
May our souls, on Thee relying,
  Find Thee still our Hope and Stay;
    By Thy mercy,
  Oh! deliver us, good Lord!

J. J. Cummins.

363.

SOULS of men, why will ye scatter
    Like a crowd of frightened sheep?
Foolish hearts, why will ye wander
    From a love so true and deep?

Was there ever kindest shepherd
    Half so gentle, half so sweet,
As the Saviour Who would have us
    Come and gather round His feet?

There's a wideness in God's mercy,
    Like the wideness of the sea;
There's a kindness in His justice,
    Which is more than liberty.

There is no place where earth's sorrows
    Are more felt than up in heaven;
There is no place where earth's failings
    Have such kindly judgment given.

There is plentiful redemption
    In the blood that has been shed;
There is joy for all the members
    In the sorrows of the Head.

For the love of God is broader
    Than the measures of man's mind;
And the heart of the Eternal
    Is most wonderfully kind.

If our love were but more simple,
    We should take Him at His word;
And our lives would be all sunshine
    In the sweetness of our Lord.

                F. W. Faber.

364.

ALLELUIA! sing to Jesus!
  His the sceptre, His the throne;
Alleluia! His the triumph,
  His the victory alone;
Hark! the songs of peaceful Sion
  Thunder like a mighty flood;
Jesus out of every nation
  Hath redeemed us by His blood.

Alleluia! not as orphans
  Are we left in sorrow now;
Allelu.a! He is near us,
  Faith believes, nor questions how:
Though the cloud from sight received Him,
  When the Forty Days were o'er,
Shall our hearts forget His promise,
  "I am with you evermore"?

Alleluia! Bread of angels,
　Thou on earth our Food, our Stay;
Alleluia! here the sinful
　Flee to Thee from day to day;
Intercessor, Friend of sinners,
　Earth's Redeemer, plead for me,
Where the songs of all the sinless
　Sweep across the crystal sea.

Alleluia! King Eternal,
　Thee the Lord of lords we own;
Alleluia! born of Mary,
　Earth Thy footstool, heaven Thy throne;
Thou within the veil hast entered,
　Robed in flesh, our great High Priest;
Thou on earth both Priest and Victim
　In the Eucharistic Feast.

Alleluia! sing to Jesus!
　His the sceptre, His the throne;
Alleluia! His the triumph,
　His the victory alone;
Hark! the songs of peaceful Sion
　Thunder like a mighty flood;
Jesus out of every nation
　Hath redeemed us by His blood.

W. C. Dix.

365.

SAVIOUR, Blessèd Saviour,
　　Listen whilst we sing,
Hearts and voices raising
　　Praises to our King;
All we have to offer,
　　All we hope to be,
Body, soul, and spirit,
　　All we yield to Thee.

Nearer, ever nearer,
　　Christ, we draw to Thee,
Deep in adoration
　　Bending low the knee:
Thou for our redemption
　　Cam'st on earth to die;
Thou, that we might follow,
　　Hast gone up on high.

Great and ever greater
　　Are Thy mercies here;
True and everlasting
　　Are the glories there;
Where no pain, nor sorrow,
　　Toil, nor care is known,
Where the angel-legions
　　Circle round Thy Throne.

Dark and ever darker
　　Was the wintry past,
Now a ray of gladness
　　O'er our path is cast;
Every day that passeth,
　　Every hour that flies,
Tells of love unfeignèd,
　　Love that never dies.

Clearer still and clearer
 Dawns the light from heaven,
In our sadness bringing
 News of sin forgiven;
Life has lost its shadows,
 Pure the light within;
Thou hast shed Thy radiance
 On a world of sin.

Brighter still and brighter
 Glows the western sun,
Shedding all its gladness
 O'er our work that's done;
Time will soon be over,
 Toil and sorrow past,
May we, Blessèd Saviour,
 Find a rest at last.

Onward, ever onward,
 Journeying o'er the road
Worn by saints before us,
 Journeying on to God;
Leaving all behind us,
 May we hasten on,
Backward never looking
 Till the prize is won.

Bliss, all bliss excelling,
 When the ransomed soul,
Earthly toils forgetting,
 Finds its promised goal;
Where in joys unheard of
 Saints with angels sing,
Never weary raising
 Praises to their King!

G. Thring.

366.

NOT for our sins alone
   Thy mercy, Lord, we sue;
Let fall Thy pitying glance
   On our devotions too,
What we have done for Thee,
   And what we think to do.

The holiest hours we spend
   In prayer upon our knees,
The times when most we deem
   Our songs of praise will please,
Thou Searcher of all hearts
   Forgiveness pour on these.

And all the gifts we bring,
   And all the vows we make,
And all the acts of love
   We plan for Thy dear sake,
Into Thy pardoning thought,
   O God of mercy, take.

And most, when we, Thy flock,
   Before Thine Altar bend,
And strange, bewildering thoughts
   With those sweet moments blend,
By Him Whose death we plead,
   Good Lord, Thy help extend.

Bow down Thine ear and hear,
   Open Thine eyes and see;
Our very love is shame,
   And we must come to Thee,
To make it of Thy grace
   What Thou would'st have it be.

H. Twells.

367.

ONE sweetly solemn thought
   Comes to me o'er and o'er;
I am nearer my home to-day
   Than I ever have been before.

Nearer the great white throne,
   Nearer the crystal sea,
Nearer my Father's house,
   Where the many mansions be.

Nearer the bound of life,
   Where we lay our burdens down;
Nearer leaving the Cross,
   Nearing gaining the Crown

But lying darkly between,
   Winding down through the night,
Is the deep and unknown stream
   To be crossed ere we reach the light.

Jesu, perfect my trust,
   Strengthen the hand of my faith:
Let me feel Thee near when I stand
   On the edge of the shore of death;

Feel Thee near when my feet
   Are slipping over the brink;
For it may be I'm nearer home,
   Nearer now than I think.

P. Cary.

368.

ONWARD, Christian soldiers,
    Marching as to war,
With the Cross of Jesus
    Going on before!
Christ the Royal Master
    Leads against the foe;
Forward into battle,
    See, His banners go.
        Onward, Christian soldiers,
            Marching as to war,
        With the Cross of Jesus
            Going on before!

At the sign of triumph
    Satan's host doth flee;
On then, Christian soldiers,
    On to victory!
Hell's foundations quiver
    At the shout of praise;
Brothers, lift your voices,
    Loud your anthems raise.
        Onward, Christian soldiers,
            Marching as to war,
        With the Cross of Jesus
            Going on before!

Like a mighty army
  Moves the Church of God;
Brothers, we are treading
  Where the saints have trod;
We are not divided,
  All one body we,
One in hope and doctrine,
  One in charity.
        Onward, Christian soldiers,
          Marching as to war,
        With the Cross of Jesus
          Going on before!

Crowns and thrones may perish,
  Kingdoms rise and wane,
But the Church of Jesus
  Constant will remain;
Gates of hell can never
  'Gainst that Church prevail;
We have Christ's own promise,
  And that cannot fail.
        Onward, Christian soldiers,
          Marching as to war,
        With the Cross of Jesus
          Going on before!

Onward, then, ye people!
  Join our happy throng,
Blend with ours your voices
  In the triumph song:
Glory, laud, and honour
  Unto Christ the King,
This through countless ages
  Men and angels sing.
        Onward, Christian soldiers,
          Marching as to war,
        With the Cross of Jesus
          Going on before!

S. Baring-Gould.

390.

THE roseate hues of early dawn,
  The brightness of the day,
The crimson of the sunset sky,
  How fast they fade away!
Oh! for the pearly gates of heaven!
  Oh! for the golden floor!
Oh! for the Sun of Righteousness
  That setteth nevermore!

The highest hopes we cherish here,
  How fast they tire and faint!
How many a spot defiles the robe
  That wraps an earthly saint!
Oh! for a heart that never sins!
  Oh! for a soul washed white!
Oh! for a voice to praise our King,
  Nor weary day or night!

Here faith is ours, and heavenly hope,
  And grace to lead us higher;
But there are perfectness and peace
  Beyond our best desire.
Oh! by Thy love and anguish, Lord,
  Oh! by Thy Life laid down,
Grant that we fall not from Thy grace,
  Nor cast away our crown!

C. F. Alexander.

391.

GUIDE us, O Thou great Jehovah,
　　Pilgrims through this barren land;
We are weak, but Thou art mighty;
　　Hold us with Thy powerful hand:
　　　　Bread of Heaven,
　　Feed us now and evermore.

Open Thou the living fountain
　　Whence the healing waters flow;
Let the fiery cloudy pillar
　　Lead us all our journey through:
　　　　Strong Deliverer,
　　Be Thou still our Strength and Shield.

When we tread the verge of Jordan,
　　Bid our anxious fears subside;
Bear us through the o'erwhelming torrent,
　　Land us safe on Canaan's side:
　　　　Songs of praises
　　We will ever give to Thee.

W. Williams.

392.

LO! God is here! let us adore
   And own how dreadful is this place!
Let all within us feel His power,
   And silent bow before His face;
Who know His power, His grace who prove,
Serve Him with awe, with reverence love.

Lo! God is here! Him day and night
   The choirs of holy angels sing;
To Him enthroned above all height
   The hosts of Heaven their praises bring;
Disdain not, Lord, our meaner song
Who praise Thee with a falt'ring tongue.

O Heavenly Father, may our praise
   Thy courts with grateful worship fill;
Still may we stand before Thy face,
   Still hear and do Thy sovereign Will;
To Thee may all our thoughts arise
A true and ceaseless sacrifice.

J. Wesley.
*(Translation from the German
of G. Tersteegen).*

INDEX OF AUTHORS.

No date is appended when the Author is believed to be living.
The Numbers affixed denote the Hymns.

INDEX OF AUTHORS.

INDEX

OF

FIRST LINES.

INDEX OF FIRST LINES.

WERTHEIMER, LEA AND CO., TYPP., CIRCUS PLACE, LONDON WALL.